BEYOND THE GREEN DOOR

Beyond the Green Door, Kristan Julius

Bjorn Again, Kathryn England

Blue Girl, Yella Fella, Bernie Monagle

Blue Murder, Ken Catran

Chenxi and the Foreigner, Sally Rippin

Cupid & Co, Carol Jones

Dear Venny, Dear Saffron, Gary Crew & Libby Hathorn

The Devil's Own, Deborah Lisson

Dreamcatcher, Jen McVeity

Edward Britton, Gary Crew & Philip Neilsen

The Eight Lives of Stullie the Great, Jim Schembri

Falling into Place, Kal Pittaway

Fat Boy Saves World, Ian Bone

Find Me a River, Bronwyn Blake

Golden Prince, Ken Catran

Gothic Hospital, Gary Crew

Hot Hits, Bernie Monagle

Killer McKenzie, Eve Martyn

A Kiss in Every Wave, Rosanne Hawke

Lifeboat, Brian Ridden

Mama's Babies, Gary Crew

Murder in Aisle 9, Jim Schembri

Not Raining Today, Wendy Catran

Operation Delta Bravo, D.J. Stutley

Operation Foxtrot Five, D.J. Stutley

Our Lady of Apollo Bay, Janine Burke

Poison under Their Lips, Mark Svendsen

Portal Bandits, Jim Schembri

The Rats of Wolfe Island, Alan Horsfield

Red Hugh, Deborah Lisson

Ridge, Dorothy Simmons

Riding the Blues, Jeri Kroll

Rock Dancer, Bronwyn Blake

Settling Storms, Charlotte Calder

Shadow across the Sun, Margaret Campbell

Silver Mantle, Gail Merritt

Snigger James on Grey, Mark Svendsen

So Much to Tell You, John Marsden

Stalker, Hazel Edwards

Sweet Tea, Brian Ridden

Talking to Blue, Ken Catran

Tin Soldiers, Ian Bone

Tomorrow the Dark, Ken Catran

Video Zone, Dorothy Simmons

Volcano Boy, Libby Hathorn

Voyage with Jason, Ken Catran

Welcome to Minute Sixteen, Jim Schembri

Whistle Man, Brian Ridden

White Lies, J.C. Burke

Wogaluccis, Josie Montano

Zenna Dare, Rosanne Hawke

BEYOND THE GREEN DOOR

KRISTAN JULIUS

Lothian
BOOKS

Dedicated to all my students
at Pattimura School who were my
'captive' audience and
to my family, especially my own Will

Thomas C. Lothian Pty Ltd
132 Albert Road, South Melbourne, Victoria 3205
www.lothian.com.au

Copyright © Kristan Julius 2002
First published 2002

National Library of Australia
Cataloguing-in-Publication data:

Julius, Kristan
Beyond the green door.

For young adults.
ISBN 0 7344 0332 1.

I. Title.

A823.4

Cover design by Michelle Mackintosh
Cover illustration by Marc McBride
Text design by Paulene Meyer
Printed in Australia by Griffin Press

PROLOGUE

Sarah was having the dream again. She knew she wouldn't remember it when she woke up; she had tried all her life and it was no use. She was standing in a large tent, across from the boy who would be a man, and more than a man, whose face was as familiar to her as her own, with his ice-grey eyes, his smirking, arrogant smile, one eyebrow elegantly lifted. His beautiful, terrifying face.

And there was the smell, foul and cloying, making Sarah choke and gag, barely able to breathe. The hooded figures behind the youth reached for her with long bony fingers, holding her in their tight grasp, their breath reeking. Sarah struggled, like always, and felt herself slipping into unconsciousness all the same.

And then came the worst part of the dream; the wailing and the unbearable pain of loss which flooded over her as she spiralled into a dark tunnel. The last sound she heard was his laugh, low and malicious, and then nothing at all.

ONE

Thunder woke Sarah. The morning was dark and rain hammered on the roof. She lay in her bed, watching the raindrops wriggle like silvery eels down the window-pane. For days, the clouds had hung heavily overhead, and now, finally, they were spilling over.

'Oh, rats!' she said aloud, and pulled the covers over her head. Aunt Jenny, her mother's sister and Sarah's favourite relative, had come all the way from Asia to stay with them until her first baby was born. She had arrived yesterday in time to celebrate Sarah's birthday.

'Today,' Sarah said within the dark huddle of her bed. 'Why does it have to rain today, on my birthday?'

They had planned a picnic in the park. Sarah had helped her mother prepare the feast the day before. They had prepared devilled eggs, potato salad and roast chickens, and Aunt Jenny had mixed up her secret tropical recipe for 'bug juice' to drink.

From beneath the covers, Sarah could hear the muffled sounds of her parents' voices in the kitchen, and light laughter. Aunt Jenny was already up! She sprang from her bed and rummaged through her drawers. She pulled on a pair of jeans and an oversized

Hard Rock Cafe t-shirt which Aunt Jenny had brought her from Singapore.

Sarah hopped into the bathroom, where she splashed her face with cool water and let it run while she brushed her teeth, smiling at herself in the mirror as she placed her toothbrush back in the rack. She pulled a comb through her hair, and examined her face for signs that she was indeed a year older. Her wide eyes were reflected back at her, her face framed by her shimmering silver hair, once considered so unusual in colour. These days people dyed their hair all sorts of shades, and Sarah enjoyed not attracting so much attention.

Do I look older? she wondered. 'I'd better,' she muttered aloud. 'This growing-up process seems to be taking its own sweet time …'

Just then there was another booming clap of thunder. Sarah headed for the hall and pounded down the stairs.

'Well,' said her father as she arrived in the kitchen, 'that's a relief! I thought we were about to be stampeded by a herd of woolly mammoths run amok!' He held out his arms and Sarah nestled into them for a morning hug.

'Woolly mammoths didn't have long silvery coats. Or did they?' said Mrs Clare as she reached across the table and tousled Sarah's hair. 'Happy birthday, sweetheart.'

'Thanks,' Sarah mumbled against her father's chest.

'Hi, Squirrel,' said Aunt Jenny. 'Can I give you a birthday hug, too?'

Sarah disentangled herself from her father's arms and gave her aunt a hard hug.

'Careful, Sarah,' said her mother. 'Remember you're hugging two people now.'

Sarah glanced anxiously at Aunt Jenny's round belly. 'I didn't hurt the baby, did I?'

Aunt Jenny smiled. 'No, honey. The baby likes your hugs, too. I'm just sorry I'm so big that I can't take you up on my lap any more.'

'Sarah's too big for laps now,' her father teased, and he reached around the table and caught her arm, drawing her up on his knees. 'OUFF!' he groaned. 'Maybe you *are* a woolly mammoth in disguise!'

Sarah giggled and nestled against him. She supposed she was getting too big to sit on laps. Today she was twelve. She breathed in her father's scent of shaving cream and coffee, and felt an unexpected pang of regret, as though she were about to lose something precious.

'Woolly mammoths are extinct, I believe,' said Sarah's mother.

'At least they died out as a result of natural selection,' said Aunt Jenny. 'Now we're the ones responsible for extinctions.'

Here we go again, thought Sarah. She adored her mother's younger sister, but she didn't have much patience with her aunt's strong views on environmental issues. It wasn't Sarah's fault that the rainforests were disappearing, and she couldn't see how she could do anything about it anyway. Once, in school, Sarah and her classmates had written letters to foreign heads of governments where rainforests were being destroyed, but she didn't think anyone ever heard back from them. She admired Aunt Jenny for her efforts, but she didn't think they would really change anything.

Sarah was distracted from her thoughts by the clatter of dishes. Her mother had deposited the dirty breakfast plates in the sink and was fiddling with the tap. 'That's funny,' Mrs Clare said. 'We don't have much pressure. Is there water running somewhere?'

'Oops,' said Sarah, as she stood up quickly. 'I think maybe I forgot to turn off the bathroom tap upstairs.'

'Oh, honey!' Aunt Jenny said, 'Water is precious. It's a crime to waste it.'

Sarah was stung by Aunt Jenny's words, even though they were spoken softly. She turned silently and headed for the stairs. When she reached the bathroom, she saw the water rushing down the drain in the basin.

'It's not that big a deal,' she grumbled to herself as she turned the tap off, but caught a glimpse of her expression in the mirror and felt ashamed of herself. She didn't want to be angry with Aunt Jenny, and she knew how hard her aunt worked to educate people about the earth's limited resources.

Sarah entered the kitchen more quietly this time.

Outside the window, there was a flash of lightning followed by the dull thud of thunder. Her aunt seemed to sense her chastened mood and gave her a warm smile.

'Sorry about the day, sweetheart,' said her mother.

'That's OK,' said Sarah, trying to hide her disappointment. She dropped onto the floor by Aunt Jenny and leaned against the chair rails. She felt her aunt's cool touch as she ran her fingers gently across Sarah's cheek.

'I like the rain,' said Aunt Jenny, drawing her long golden hair up on top of her head. 'You've had such a hot, dry summer. Besides,' she continued, 'who says a birthday picnic has to be outside?'

Sarah and her parents looked at Aunt Jenny expectantly. She was always full of surprises and ready for adventures. She lived halfway around the world at a rainforest research station with Uncle Dan, where they worked to try to save the jungles there from destruction. Sarah thought her aunt was the bravest person in the world. She loved to look at the photographs of the animals and plants that lived around Aunt Jenny's home. She was waiting impatiently to be thirteen, when her parents had promised her they would let her travel there to see the rainforest for herself.

Only one more year now, thought Sarah as she smiled up at her aunt.

'Let's go …' Aunt Jenny began, as she breathed

deeply and looked up, studying the ceiling as if she might find a map there.

Sarah found that she was holding her breath.

'I've got it!' Aunt Jenny cried, and she rose out of her chair and spread her arms. 'I know a perfect picnic place to celebrate this fine rainy day!'

'Where?' asked Sarah.

Aunt Jenny's green eyes twinkled. 'That,' she smiled, 'is the surprise!'

An hour later they were all in the hot house at City Botanical Gardens. Aunt Jenny's friend Seth worked there and was delighted to host the gathering and join in the feast. Seth's contribution to the celebration included a guided tour of the tropical plants. He walked them down the aisles of the greenhouses, naming the strange and beautiful vegetation for them.

'This is a philodendron, and those are bamboo,' Seth said, pointing to a clump of slender trees.

'Every year we see so many species disappear,' Aunt Jenny said sadly, fingering a velvety poinsettia leaf. 'It's frightening.'

Sarah wandered on ahead. The green house was pretty, but she wished the rain would stop and she could go outside. She felt confined in the humid building, surrounded by all the plants.

After inspecting the greenhouses, they returned

to Seth's office and devoured the picnic lunch beneath a banana tree in his cramped work space. Sarah breathed in the steamy air full of subtle aromas. 'Cinnamon and spice,' she murmured drowsily. The sound of the sprinklers made her sleepy. She was lulled by the voices of the adults, and slightly bored by all the talk about 'environmental issues'. She stood up and stretched, and then wandered back into the main greenhouse, reading the little signs as she walked down the row of plants. Deep pink flowers adorned a bush with terrible spikes. There were many kinds of ferns with feathery-fingered fronds, and plants with leaves like large tongues.

'Elephant ears,' Sarah pronounced as she examined a broad leaf that dangled in her path. She brushed past it and imagined herself in the depths of a real jungle. Vines curled from a tree branch above her and she shivered at the thought of snakes. She didn't like reptiles of any kind.

Near the back of the building, she discovered a small green door that she hadn't noticed during their previous tour. From a distance it appeared quite ordinary and, because of its colour, it was almost hidden in the overhanging leaves, but as she approached it, she saw that it was rather interesting.

In the centre of the door was a gold serpent, its coils twisted into a knocker of sorts. As Sarah peered more closely, the snake's skin seemed to shimmer and quiver; startled, she stood up abruptly, knocking her head on a low-hanging clay pot. Wincing from the pain, she tripped forward and grasped the knocker for support.

As she touched the snake, several things seemed to happen at once.

The face of the door began to change. Designs appeared, revealing the shapes of wild cats with golden eyes, and soaring bats, fierce boars and scampering monkeys amid swooping parrots of coral red. She heard waves upon a shore like the echo of a seashell against her ear, then the sound of a feral cat growling in the distance.

Sarah felt the green door begin to vibrate as all the wondrous creatures danced across it. And then slowly, the door was swinging open, revealing not the outside street or a greenhouse aisle, but a rushing river of water, which stretched beyond Sarah's vision. Sarah turned to look behind her, to the safety of the work space down the end of the aisle, the real world, but as she did so, she felt herself falling forward into the swirling waters.

TWO

Sarah closed her eyes as the monstrous river rose to meet her, but instead of the cold splash she expected, she landed with a bump on soft dusty ground. The sound of the river faded to a murmur and she opened her eyes to find she was sitting under a scraggly gnarled tree.

In front of her crouched a small boy, studying her intently. For several heartbeats, Sarah said nothing as she struggled to catch her breath. The boy continued to watch her, and finally Sarah felt she had to say something.

'Well, what are you looking at?' she said, more sharply than she intended. The boy's clear eyes relaxed and he smiled so merrily that Sarah felt some of her panic melting away. 'Um … hello,' she said. 'Do you know … I mean … could you tell me where we are?' she asked, in what she hoped was a more polite tone.

'We're in Karst, in the land of Hutanya,' replied the boy, and now it was Sarah's turn to stare, for the boy's voice was marvellous to hear, like a capering brook dancing over smooth stones.

'I know who you are,' the boy continued. 'You've come to free the waters!'

'Excuse me?' Sarah replied. She was only half listening. The boy's voice spilled over her, cool and refreshing, although the sun was high and Sarah saw that they were surrounded by the sandy terrain of a desert. She felt oddly calm … until she looked behind her and saw the faint outline of the green door shimmer in the heat before fading completely. She gasped in dismay. Where was she?

The boy was standing now and dusting sand from his hands.

'We'd best be off,' he said, 'before they discover you've arrived. Although they might not know who you are.' The boy did a graceful spin, lightly sprinkling Sarah with a fine mist.

'Who I am?' repeated Sarah. 'How would you know who I am? You don't even know my name.'

The boy grinned at her. 'You're Sareka!'

Sarah felt an odd tingling up her spine as he said the strange name. She shook her head. 'No, my name is not … whatever you said. My name is Sarah, and I'm a bit confused right now.' She looked around at the vast dry land surrounding them. 'Make that very confused.'

The boy said nothing, but sat patiently before her, with his sunny smile still in place.

'Look,' said Sarah. 'Let's start again. I'm Sarah, Sarah Clare, actually.'

The boy stood up and bowed solemnly. He said, 'I'm Will. Just Will, and we've been waiting for you a long, long time.'

'For me?' Sarah said in surprise. 'But you don't even know me!' she repeated. She looked around again at the dry harsh landscape. 'I'm afraid I don't understand any of this. And my head aches terribly.' She put her hand up to feel a rising lump on the back of her skull.

Instantly, Will was beside her, examining the bump. His eyes were like green pools. He laid his hand gently on her head and again Sarah felt the coolness rising from his touch. His voice was full of concern. 'You've hurt yourself. Here,' he said, as he dusted smooth a space in the sand, 'lie back and rest awhile.'

Sarah obeyed, resting her head on her hands. 'Please, Will, can you start at the beginning? How did I get here? For that matter, where is here? And what makes you think I was supposed to come?'

'So many questions!' Will said with the grin which Sarah was beginning to find slightly maddening. He shook himself and Sarah was astonished to see a rainbow rise and arc around him. Small green sprouts sprang from the sand where he stood, and withered almost immediately in the heat.

'How did you do …?' Sarah began, and then words failed her.

Will appeared not to notice as he began to explain. 'We're in Karst, in the heart of Hutanya, which is now wasteland, although it wasn't always like this. There was once a great rainforest here.'

Sarah gazed at the arid desert. Turning her head

made it throb painfully. 'Hard to believe,' she murmured. 'What happened to the forest?'

'An army of spirit beings invaded our land,' replied Will. 'We call them the dry wraiths. They have collected most of the water that once ran so plentifully here, for their master, Sarin.' Will shuddered as he said the name. 'He is a dark sorcerer who lives now in the northern lands. Sarin is responsible for the great loss of life in Hutanya in the past twelve years. Once he was Marwa's apprentice, until the evil within him was discovered. His thirst for power is unquenchable. Marwa says that Sarin has been deliberately killing off everything and everyone. Sarin uses the wraiths because he hasn't the power yet to destroy life directly. He takes the water instead, but the outcome is the same.'

The boy paused and Sarah saw a look of worry crease his perfect brow. Then he caught her gaze and smiled again. 'Or would be the same, if you hadn't come.'

Sarah struggled to sit up to protest, but the sharp pain as she moved her head silenced her.

'I am here,' Will continued, 'because after the waters disappeared, I was sent by the Old Magic. Don't ask me from where because I don't remember. My first memory is of sitting right here under this tree. Marwa says I am a wish waiting to happen.' He smiled at the puzzled look on Sarah's face. 'I don't know what he means either. You,' he said looking deeply into

Sarah's eyes, 'have come to free the waters. That is all I know.'

Sarah sat up in alarm. 'How can you be so sure I have anything to do with all this?'

'Because,' Will said, 'you came through the green door. That's how it's written.'

'Written where?' asked Sarah. 'And who is Marwa?' She closed her eyes in an attempt to ease the pain that pounded in her temples, and felt Will's cool hand lightly touch her forehead.

When Sarah opened her eyes again, she was alone. The day was fading into dusk. She felt the gritty scrunch of sand on her arms and legs. Her headache was gone, but her throat was parched and dry. She gazed up at the brown shrivelled leaves of the ancient tree which stirred in the tepid breeze.

A cool shadow fell over her. 'Here,' said Will, offering her a woven bag, 'drink this.'

Sarah tipped her head obediently. The water filled her mouth, cold and delicious. Will's small solemn face leaned close to hers. He reminded her of someone, with his deep green eyes. He looked so concerned that she giggled and choked a bit on the water, and he responded with laughter spilling from him.

'Where did you go before?' Sarah asked, handing him the water bag. 'And where did you get this water?'

She felt too relieved to be really upset with him for disappearing. The cool water had filled her with lightness.

'Go?' asked Will. 'I didn't go anywhere. You fell asleep. And I brought the water with me from the caves. I've been on watch. They move so quietly, you know … But now it's our time!' he crowed. 'I'll bet they're afraid!'

Sarah struggled up, brushing the sand from her hands and legs.

'Please,' she said, ' who are *they*? You're still talking in riddles.'

Will looked at her with solemn eyes. 'But I thought you'd know what to do,' he said quietly.

'About what?' Sarah felt exasperation rising within her.

'About the dry wraiths, about freeing the waters, about wishes …' Will's voice trailed off uncertainly.

'Look,' said Sarah, as she ruffled her hands through her hair, 'all I know is that I fell against a door in the greenhouse, into a river which turned to sand, and then met you, a water baby of some sort, who talks utter nonsense!'

In her agitation, Sarah gave her head one final shake and gasped as a small lizard dropped from the tangles of her hair. She let out a yelp and leapt back.

Will's troubled gaze melted into a smile. 'It's Ashrok! Hello, little fellow!'

The lizard rolled its yellow eyes and flicked its tongue, snatching a small insect from the dusty air. It croaked once, a deep sound for so small a creature, and rolled its eyes again. Sarah took a cautious step backward.

'Oh, of course!' cried Will. He turned, spraying Sarah with mist, and grasped her hand. 'We must go to the caves!' He stopped and asked, 'Can you read?'

'Of course I can read,' Sarah sputtered, but before she could say more, she found herself fairly galloping along beside Will across the open plain, the sand so hot she could feel it burn through her shoes. She soon discovered that if she ran in Will's shadow the heat didn't touch her, because of the fine spray that rose from his body.

'Where …?' she gulped, but the words were snatched from her mouth by the speed of their passage, and she decided to save her questions until they slowed their pace.

Out of the corner of her eye, Sarah saw a flicker and realised the lizard was wriggling along beside her at incredible speed. She hoped he wouldn't decide to hitch a ride in her hair again.

The plain seemed to stretch endlessly before them, and Sarah was gathering her energy to ask Will to stop and rest, when suddenly, rising ahead of them, she saw great orange cliffs, their faces pitted with deep cracks and fissures. The cliffs shimmered in the late afternoon heat, and Sarah wondered for a moment if they were a mirage. They cast long shadows, like gigantic fingers, as Will and Sarah approached.

'We're almost there,' called Will, as he darted ahead, and Sarah followed the trail of sprouts and tendrils of green which sprang up in his footsteps.

The cliffs seemed to loom suddenly close, and as Sarah slowed her pace she gazed up at the crags and great scars in the rock. High atop them, she thought she saw something move, a puff of grey that might have been a low cloud, except that the sky above was clear. She blinked and looked again, but there was nothing there.

'Oh, well,' she muttered to herself, 'why shouldn't I be seeing things? Everything is all turned around.' They loped right up to the high cliffs and, just as Sarah opened her mouth to ask Will where they were going, she was startled to see him slipping through a small opening in the rocks.

'Hey,' she called, 'hey, wait for me!'

She approached the hole and peered inside. It was pitch black. A hint of coolness drifted out to her.

'Like Alice,' she thought, 'down the rabbit's hole.' She drew a tremulous breath and stepped inside.

THREE

At first, Sarah could see nothing. The space around her seemed infinite, and there were rustling sounds coming from somewhere above her head. She put an invisible hand out in front of her and cautiously took a few steps forward. The ground beneath her feet felt sticky.

'Will?'

The sound of her own voice startled her. A faint lightening off to her left drew her slowly forward. Her hand struck a damp wall, and something dripped down from above, making soft plopping noises around her feet. She moved quickly ahead and the darkness brightened to grey.

'Where are you?' she whispered. She felt along the wall until it ended abruptly. She could just make out the outline of her fingers.

'Will!' she called, and her voice ricocheted off invisible stone. She groped blindly forward, almost stumbling in her haste, and rounded the wall.

Blinking in the sudden light, what she saw made her gasp in wonder. She had entered a vast cavern, lit from the far side by blazing torches set into the stone wall. Stalactites hung from the high ceiling and sparkled with a dazzling brightness.

The walls were covered with paintings of birds and beasts, so real they appeared to soar and leap. Running in circles and pentagons around the creatures were curious symbols. It was a huge mural, a lush jungle painted on frozen waterfalls of rock. Sarah had never seen anything so wonderful.

'So!' The sound of Will's voice made her start. She saw him crouched beneath one of the torches, an impish grin on his face. 'Now, you can read!'

Sarah stared back at him, unable to find her voice.

'No, I think not,' said another voice, so deep that it made Sarah tremble. She saw a tall figure dimly outlined just beyond the torchlight. The silhouette moved forward, revealing a man with a face so deeply lined that it reminded Sarah of the cliffs outside. She thought he must be a million years old. The flickering light struck his eyes as his cloudy blue gaze turned towards Sarah. He studied her as if he were trying to read her.

'I think,' the tall man continued, 'that you are mistaken, my little friend.' He took another step forward and Sarah instinctively moved back. He did not look at all friendly. She shifted her eyes to Will. His happy smile wavered uncertainly, and then flickered brightly again.

'Of course I'm not wrong,' the boy cried. 'Come on,' he urged. 'Read!'

Sarah felt irritation replacing her apprehension. 'Read?' she asked. 'Read what?'

The torchlight sputtered. Will suddenly looked bleak, and he seemed to grow smaller.

'The runes,' he said softly. 'Read the runes.'

Before Sarah could ask what runes were, the old man spoke.

'She cannot,' he said gently. 'Don't lose heart, boy. I don't know who she is, but she's not the one.'

'I can read,' said Sarah. 'But I don't see any words.'

'It's none of your concern,' the man said brusquely, and he laid a hand on Will's shoulder. 'Go back to wherever you came from. Leave this place.' He waved his hand in Sarah's direction, and started to turn away.

Sarah felt a sudden anger rising over her fear. 'Gladly!' she said, and the force of her voice rang through the cavern. 'I'd be very happy to leave, to be home. I don't know who you are or how I got here, and I'm very tired of riddles, but I don't know how to leave.'

The old man's blue eyes flashed, and then studied her again.

'Well, whoever she is, she doesn't lack spirit,' he murmured.

'And I'll thank you,' Sarah retorted, 'to stop referring to me as *she!*'

Amusement replaced the hard look in the old man's eyes. 'And how would my Lady like to be addressed?'

'My name is Sarah Clare,' she said, blushing furiously.

The old man stared. 'Say your name again.'

'I don't ...' began Sarah, but the old man silenced her with a swift downward movement of his great hand.

'Say it!' he commanded.

Sarah drew herself up and said in a clear, steady voice, 'Sarah. My name is Sarah Clare.'

'Sareka!' he whispered and at the sound of his voice, the creatures on the walls seemed to stir. 'Can it be?'

Sarah felt the cavern tremble around her, as if the animals in the paintings had been set in motion and were thundering in her direction. The glistening stalactites and stalagmites seemed to yawn and stretch towards her like fangs, and the floor beneath her tilted until she pitched forward. She threw out her hands to break her fall and felt, instead of the treacherous bite of the stalagmites, strong arms cradle her. Then there was only darkness.

Sarah was aware of a whispering flapping that sent a breeze across her face. She opened her eyes. She was surrounded by bats, their sharp faces tempered by large, soulful eyes. They hovered above her, slowly fanning their wings, creating the stirring air. As she blinked, preparing to scream, one of the creatures swooped closer, its pointy snout nearly brushing her nose.

'Don't be afraid,' it squeaked. 'We are batlings. You fainted, and Marwa instructed us to guard you until you awoke. Archana will tell him you have revived.'

A small batling with long curling eyelashes flitted off into the cavern depths.

Sarah breathed slowly, trying to calm her pounding heart. She was in a cave. She was lying on a bed of dried grasses. With talking bats. She peered into the eyes of the hovering creature and sensed no malice in them.

'Please,' whispered Sarah, struggling to sit up, 'can you answer some questions?'

The batling swung itself upside down, and gained a perch on the ceiling directly above Sarah's head.

'Ahhh,' he sighed, 'with pleasure. What would you like to know?'

Sarah cleared her throat. *What would she like to know? She was talking to a bat!*

'All right,' she began, 'let's start with who you are and where we are.'

'My name is Calum, and this is Karst, the cave world of Hutanya. We are the last remaining inhabitants here. There are also the Dasai, a tribe of people who live on the High Plains. And the Godawa are nomads who live to the south of here, but there are few waterholes left on their lands. The rest …' The batling shrugged his wings.

'Go on,' said Sarah. 'The rest …?'

'The rest,' said the batling, 'is wasteland.'

Calum's words set the cavern flapping, a whirring unrest that created a sea of wind.

'We don't speak often about what happened to Hutanya,' Calum explained, as the flurry died down. 'The dry wraiths, servants of Sarin, help him by finding and draining all the water we have. Their thirst is insatiable, and it is said they exist in constant torment, craving water day and night. No one knows where the wraiths came from, but Sarin is a powerful sorcerer, so perhaps he conjured them up. He waits in the mountains to the north, holding the waters there in his freezing grip. The Great Falls, the source of our waters, are locked in ice by his dark magic.'

'I'm sorry,' said Sarah, 'but what has all this to do with me?'

The batling paused to ponder her question. 'For one thing,' said Calum, 'I am certain that Sarin will not stop with this world. Some say he has already begun a force in the world beyond the green door, your world. Power seeks power. Once Sarin controls Hutanya, he will look for ways to expand his empire. It is said that in your world there is a lot of water, but that your people don't care so much about it. Then there is, of course, your legacy.'

'My what?' asked Sarah.

At that moment, Archana returned. 'Marwa awaits you,' she said.

Calum blinked his large brown eyes. 'Marwa can best answer that question, but I will tell you this. Your name is sacred here, Sareka.'

The unpleasant feeling rose again like a bad taste in her mouth. 'Why?' she managed to whisper.

'Because,' replied Calum, swooping down from his perch to hover in front of her, 'you are our last hope.'

FOUR

The batling led Sarah through a series of long tunnels to another cavern. Here, water had worked its magic as well. Ripples of cave draperies adorned the entrance, and torches set discreetly in recesses in the walls illuminated the magnificent rock formations that decorated the cave. Sarah was reminded of a cathedral she had once visited with Aunt Jenny, with its arching ceiling and towering columns.

She stared at the murals on the walls. They were so realistic, she felt she could almost smell the jungle flowers and hear the rustling of the high forest canopy. She caught sight of Will standing against one of the dripping walls and wanted to call out to him, but the majesty of the place held her silent. Solemnly he placed the torch he was carrying in a large sconce and then flashed his sudden grin and skipped towards her. Sarah was aware again of his coolness, as he knelt before her and lifted his small, shining face.

'Hello, Sareka,' he said, smiling shyly.

Beyond him Sarah saw a stirring of light and Marwa appeared. He was dressed in robes of forest green, studded with constellations of shimmering silver. He raised his arms four times towards the corners of the cavern, his eyes closed, murmuring to himself, and then beckoned to the children. Still silent, he indicated that they should sit on the richly embroidered cushions at his feet. Sarah felt his power, but this time she was not afraid. He settled before them and took both their hands, small in his great grasp.

'Forgive me,' he said quietly, and Sarah was surprised to see the warmth in his strange frosted eyes. 'It's just that I didn't expect you would be so … so young. Just as when you left us.' He shook his head slowly, and Sarah thought she saw the glint of tears in his eyes. She raised her head to speak, but he said, 'Hear me first. And then I will answer your questions.' He turned and surveyed the walls of the cavern. He seemed to grow as he gazed at them, to gain strength from the vivid murals painted there.

'First,' he said, 'yes, there is a way home for you. Secondly, your family and friends will not miss you, at least if your mission here is accomplished.'

'But how …?' asked Sarah, and then she caught her lip between her teeth and completed her thought silently. *How can Marwa know my questions if I haven't asked them yet?*

'Time has a different rhythm here,' Marwa explained. 'What might take moons to accomplish in Hutanya will be but several blinks of an eye in your world. There is much you will need to learn while you stay with us in Karst. The batlings and I will instruct you, for it is apparent that your knowledge is sleeping and there may not be time for you to come to a full awakening here. Calum and Archana will accompany you to the Teeth, and along the way they will have to guide you in whatever I have not been able to teach you before you must depart.'

Sarah opened her mouth to protest. *Depart? And go where?* But she did not speak, for somewhere within her was stirring an older memory, and she found its voice irresistible. She felt that all of this, frightening and impossible as it seemed, was also somehow familiar, and she was prepared to listen and wait. She heard a faint rustling overhead, and looked up to find the two batlings roosting, blinking their bright eyes shyly at her. She found their presence reassuring.

'You won't be alone on your quest,' piped Will. 'I shall go as well.'

'No,' said Marwa fiercely. 'I cannot risk it.' Seeing Will's face fall, he added more gently, 'There is much for you to do here, my small friend.'

'But I found her!' persisted Will. 'Surely I can claim my right to accompany her, at least,' he added hastily, seeing Marwa's brows draw together, 'at least across the High Plain to the foothills of the Teeth.' His upturned face was full of hope, and Sarah had to smile at his persuasive eyes, despite the nervous churning in her stomach.

There was a long silence before Marwa stroked Will's cheek and said gruffly, 'I suppose it is your right. I had hoped to keep you by me for the time remaining to …' He sighed and Sarah saw his broad shoulders stoop, as if under some burden. 'So be it,' he said, 'but only to the Teeth. And you must promise to guard yourself well.'

'Oh, I will!' cried the boy, and the air around him seemed to shimmer as he settled happily again at the old man's feet.

Marwa focused his gaze again upon Sarah. 'I know all this is strange to you. You are right to feel frightened. Your appearance back in Hutanya is a mystery, as was your disappearance. The task ahead is …' The sorcerer's voice trailed off as he glanced with concern at Will.

Calum's last words to Sarah echoed in her mind. *Your name is sacred here.* Somehow, for some reason, she was here in Hutanya. Beneath all her confusion and fear something stirred, some older sense. A sudden resolve came over her.

'I'll go,' she said, before she could stop to think.

The old wizard looked back at her intently, saying nothing.

'I'm sure,' she said. 'I'll go.'

And so Marwa proceeded to guide Sarah in what he called her awakening.

'This land was once a great forest, home to many birds and beasts,' the sorcerer began, after they had made themselves comfortable with steaming glasses of herb tea. 'The batlings, lizards and small insects are all that remain of the vast population that was once Hutanya. The rest died out as the waters were stolen, the dry wraiths sucking the very life from this place. The survivors were driven to the caves, and the last reservoirs, with the exception of the few oases in the southern lands and the water pools on the High Plains in the north, are here. The great waterfall of the Teeth, which once filled the waterways of Hutanya, is locked in ice and snow under the spell of Sarin. It is possible that any day now he will discover the remaining reservoirs and send his wraiths to siphon them dry.' The wizard paused to take a sip of tea, and then reached over and patted Sarah's hand gently. 'I know you have many questions. It is important that you do not come too quickly to awakening. After rest, I will tell you who you are, Sareka. For now I will tell you this.' Marwa looked deeply into Sarah's eyes. 'Unless you can defeat Sarin and free the captive waters in his frozen grip, the last of Hutanyan life will be lost.'

'But how?' Sarah asked. 'And why me?'

Will turned to her. 'You came through the door. The green door. Just as it has been written.' He pointed to the symbols which ran riot through the jungles painted on the cave walls. 'Read the runes for her, Marwa.'

Without looking at the symbols, Marwa quoted, *'And it shall be she who comes from beyond the green door who will strike the desert back and set the waters free.'* There is much more, but I have forgotten, and the last of the readers in Karst is gone. Only I remain, and Will, whom I have been attempting to instruct.'

'Then why don't you read the, what do you call them … runes?' asked Sarah. Will glanced quickly at Sarah and made a small gesture towards his eyes, shaking his head silently.

'Because,' said Marwa, 'I cannot. In my last struggle with Sarin, I was struck by his rod. He touched my eyes. I am nearly blind.'

Later as they prepared for sleep in a small alcove, Sarah asked Will, 'Why does he call me Sareka?' She felt uneasy whispering the strange name. Each time she did, the walls seemed to tilt slightly, and the creatures and plants in the murals seemed to stir.

'Because that's who you are. Marwa will explain tomorrow, I'm sure,' said Will, as he nestled into the dry grasses laid for their bedding. He yawned and murmured, 'I guess Sarah is what they call you in your world, but the one who comes through the green door is Sareka, and you came through the door, so …' his voice trailed off sleepily.

'Will,' Sarah said, 'who is Sarin, this dark sorcerer? Have you ever met him?' She raised herself up on one elbow. She saw, to her irritation, that Will had already fallen asleep. Curled into a ball, he seemed small and vulnerable.

'Will,' she whispered loudly.

He smiled, but did not answer, and let out a gentle snore.

It was difficult to tell how long she lay awake before she became aware of movement. The cave was illuminated by a single torch which sputtered and sent shadows dancing across the walls. She studied the animals that clung to trees and crept beneath the understorey on the forest floor. Gradually she realised that the caves were a record, a great painted vault of the life that had once existed in this place. Two monkey-like creatures clung to a limb, eating a strange yellow fruit; below them great boars foraged for food in the brush, two of them with spiralled tusks. Birds of brilliant reds and greens flitted in and out of the trees, and giant butterflies with tiny eyes dipped long tongues into blossoms. Speckled cats were draped over branches, their luminous teeth glowing, and there were many other creatures unlike any animal Sarah had ever seen. There were trees with great purple fruits, shrubs with blossoms like lips about to be kissed, and small plants covered with outlandish spikes that looked like punk hairstyles. There were two of each kind.

She sensed movement, but nothing moved. It was more a stirring, like breathing, that seemed to fill the cavern with a soft breeze. Looking up, she saw that the two batlings were slowly fanning their wings as they slept. Calum hummed softly and Archana stretched out a long winged finger to gently stroke his furry back. The humming stopped, and Sarah smiled. She remembered a bad dream that had made her cry out, and her father's gentle voice calming her, taking away the fear and sending her back to sleep. She wondered about her parents and Aunt Jenny. What were they doing? Were they looking for her? Were they worried? Did they even know that she was gone? A sharp pang of homesickness struck her and tears welled up in her eyes. She muffled a sob.

In an instant, Will was awake, and peering at her anxiously. 'What is it?' he asked. 'Are you crying?'

'No,' said Sarah, feeling embarrassed by his attention. 'It's only a few tears.'

'You needn't be afraid,' the boy said softly. 'I'll protect you. I imagine, being Sareka, you won't need much protection, but I'll do my best.' And before Sarah could say another word, he was off to sleep again.

'I can take care of myself,' Sarah replied grumpily to his sleeping form. But despite her irritation, she, too, finally fell asleep.

FIVE

'Sareka,' whispered Will. 'Are you asleep?'

'Not any more,' said Sarah. 'What time is it?' Looking around the cavern, she noticed that new torches had been lit, and the cavern glowed in their flickering light.

'Time to continue your awakening,' said Marwa, smiling down at her from behind Will.

Sarah yawned and stretched. 'Even when I'm dreaming,' she muttered, 'I have to get up and go to school!'

Marwa's face grew solemn. 'It's no dream, Sareka. You are back with us again. Come, drink,' he said kindly. He held out a steaming cup.

Sarah rose and accepted the tea from the wizard. She sipped it and felt warmth spread to her toes.

Will had settled down beside Marwa. He patted the cushion next to him, and Sarah sat.

'Let me tell you,' began the old man, 'what I can. I know that you are Sareka, a young sorceress of Hutanya, who disappeared over twelve years ago.'

'What do you mean, disappeared?' asked Sarah. She felt goosebumps rising on her skin.

'Sarin was not so powerful then, or so we

believed. I had discovered him using Dark Magic, and had sent him away from Hutanya. We had news that he was destroying water holes in the south.' Marwa grew silent, and Sarah saw that heavy look of sadness on his face again.

'What happened, Marwa?' she said softly.

'You, Sareka, were young, but wise beyond your years. I thought it was time for you to test your powers. I sent you to deal with him. Alone.' The old man shook his head. 'What a fool I was!'

Will drew close to Marwa and gently touched his arm. 'You are the wisest one in the world,' the boy said.

Marwa smiled at Will. 'I've learned a few lessons since then, but they were at a terrible cost.' He continued with his story. 'Weeks passed, and there was no word. Then Tor came with the news that the council members of Godawan elders, who had met to determine Sarin's guilt or innocence, were all spirit-sick. They had been touched by wraiths and were not expected to recover.'

'What about Sareka?' asked Sarah, who could not bring herself to believe she had any connection with the sorceress.

'Gone. Without a trace. As I said, you simply disappeared.'

Sarah felt a tingling down her spine and shivered. 'And you say all this happened twelve years ago?' Her eyes widened as a thought struck her. 'Then that was just before I was …'

But Marwa wasn't listening. His tired eyes looked into the distance as he remembered the past. 'It all happened so quickly after that. Sarin marched across the southern lands with his growing army of wraiths, horrid creatures who sprang from evil, Sarin's evil, I'm sure. They sucked the waters dry with their thirsty mouths, and the skies were hazy with clouds of vile-smelling steam from their breath. There were many small tribes here in the rainforest. They tried, too late, to resist the wraiths. They had lived in peace together since the beginning of memory, and they knew nothing of war. There wasn't much fighting.' Marwa's gaze shifted inward as he remembered. 'Without water, they grew weak. Some tribes, like the Minak who lived in this area, surrendered, believing that Sarin would show them mercy. They were wrong.'

The crackling of the torch was the only sound in the huge cavern. Sarah didn't want to know how the Minak people had died. She looked uneasily at Will. He seemed to understand that she wanted to stop Marwa from telling them what horrors had occurred.

'But the Godawa and Dasai survived,' said Will.

'The Godawa, under Tor, were one of the two strongest tribes. Tor went alone, and made a bargain with Sarin.'

'What sort of a bargain?' asked Sarah.

The old man gave a weak smile. 'Tor offered to provide scouts to hunt out the hidden reserves of water in the dying forest. In exchange, Sarin agreed not to come back to Godawaland. The wraiths had already marched through those arid lands. Sarin didn't feel he needed to go back.' Marwa shook his head slowly. 'It is a terrible story, this one. I am sorry to burden you with it.'

It *was* a terrible story, thought Sarah, but one she had to know. 'Go on, Marwa. Then what happened?'

'Without water, it was only a matter of months before the land became unrecognisable. The jungles, and all life within them, shrivelled and died, winds blew away the soil and left what you saw when you first arrived. Desert. The only living things that remain in Karst are those plants and animals that can eke out an almost waterless existence, and those of us who became the hidden cave dwellers.'

'Are there other survivors here with you?' asked Sarah.

Marwa sighed, and Sarah was stricken to see large tears rolling unchecked down the old man's cheeks. 'There were. We were not many, but too many to be supported by the caves. It was agreed that some would try to reach the Dasai in the north. I was against this plan, but other younger voices were more convincing. In the end, because families did not wish to be parted, they all left. We have heard nothing of them since.'

'But you stayed, Marwa?' asked Sarah. 'Why?'

'To guard the murals,' said the wizard, sweeping his arm out towards the paintings that covered the walls. 'To keep the records of Hutanya safe.'

The children turned to study the towering jungle on the rock, and Sarah was struck once more by how realistic it was.

Marwa continued. 'There was a great battle on the High Plains, and Sarin was driven to the east by Rein, the leader of the Dasai. Rein was not much more than a boy at the time, scarcely older than you, Sareka, but a mighty warrior and a son of the sons of the Old Magic as well. Of course, Sarin was even …' Marwa paused suddenly, and averted his eyes. He cleared his throat and continued. 'Sarin retreated to the north where he used what remained of his powers to seal the last of the waters under his sorcery, by locking them in ice and snow. It was there, in the frozen mountains, that Sarin went to lick his wounds and gather his strength before attempting his final assault on the last reserves of Hutanya. I believe that time has come. My inner sight tells me that Sarin has somehow managed to become even more powerful. I do not think Rein or anyone else can stand in his way now.' Marwa turned to Sarah, his eyes fierce and penetrating, despite their milky glaze. 'Except you, Sareka.'

'Except me,' Sarah echoed faintly. *I'm supposed to be a great sorceress? I don't even have the power to scream right now!*

'Rein will meet you when you reach the grasslands and provide you with an escort to the Teeth.'

'The Teeth,' repeated Sarah, beginning to feel like a parrot.

'This is the name given to the treacherous mountains in the northlands where Sarin has mustered his troops of wraiths, and where the frozen waters of Hutanya are held. For the time being, I will instruct you in the runes and try to assist you as you awaken to your older self, Sareka. We will speak of the past, and I will do what I can to help you remember,' said Marwa.

'I think that will be a big job,' said Sarah, 'since I don't seem to remember anything.'

Marwa smiled and gently patted her hand. 'Perhaps this is not such a terrible thing,' he murmured.

It wasn't until much later that Sarah realised what the wizard meant.

Looking back, Sarah would not remember if days or weeks elapsed before they embarked on their journey to the Teeth. The days that followed were full, divided by changes in the torchlight. Sarah and Will would awaken to a brilliantly lit cavern, breakfast on seeds and the fruit of desert plants, and spend their mornings with the batlings, who had made the journey before, learning about the signs that would guide them and the dangers to avoid along the way.

Marwa always visited them at their mid-day meal, which consisted of the pulp of cactus-like plants and bittersweet scrub grasses that could be served in many ways. The cactus was palatable to Sarah, succulent and nutty-tasting, but she found the grasses incredibly stringy and hard to chew, and ate them only because Marwa glowered at her when she first complained of her distaste for them.

'They have great value for your health,' he grumbled, and Sarah was reminded of her grandfather the first time he had served her steamed clams and she had turned her nose up at them. So she munched away unhappily, forcing herself to swallow.

'What do you call this stuff, anyway?' she asked Will in a low voice after choking down a few mouthfuls.

'Chevis,' he replied, crunching happily. 'Delicious, isn't it?'

'No,' said Sarah, 'it isn't. It tastes like horsehair.'

'What is horsehair?' asked Will, who was always eager to learn about Sarah's world.

'It's part of an animal. This tastes like the tail, the back part that hangs down from its rump.' Sarah cast her eyes on a pony-like creature that seemed to prance across the cave wall. 'Sort of like that,' she said, nodding towards the mural.

Will followed her gaze and his face split into a wide grin. He choked, laughing, and Sarah pounded him on the back. When he had recovered his breath, he said, 'That is a chevis!'

'Is that what I'm eating?' gasped Sarah in horror.

Will threw back his head and laughed loudly. 'Of

course not! We don't eat animals!' he cried. 'It's just that the grasses are like, like …'

'The tail of a chevis,' finished Sarah, and she put her bowl aside in disgust. 'Yuck!'

'What is yuck?' asked Will.

Exasperated, Sarah snapped, 'This awful food!'

Later that evening they were studying the runes with Marwa, dutifully reciting the meanings of the signs he made on clay tablets and then searching for them on the cavern walls. Sarah privately thought it was a waste of time, since there were so many of them, and it was apparent that she could not possibly learn them all before they must set out on the journey to the mountains in the north. Still, she liked the lessons. She had always been quick to learn, and Marwa was an excellent, if demanding, teacher. He made the lessons interesting, bringing the legends of the ancient forest of Hutanya to life.

'It's important that you learn to read as many of the runes as time allows,' the wizard said. 'They may serve to guide you on your journey to the final confrontation with Sarin.'

Sarah didn't like the sound of the word *confrontation*. She didn't feel capable of having even a disagreement with an evil sorcerer! 'What about the other tribes?' she asked. 'Can they read the runes?'

Marwa smiled proudly. 'You ask good questions, Sareka. Yes, there are a few people who still remember. Rein, certainly, and Tor. But we have had little contact with them since the last raids of the wraiths. It is dangerous to travel now, and those who know of these caves here stay away for fear of leading the dry wraiths to us. The batlings alone still venture out and bring back news of the desert and the High Plains.'

'What about Will?' asked Sarah, and as she glanced at him she saw a sheepish grin appear on his face.

'Will goes out without my permission,' Marwa replied sternly, but his voice held no real anger. 'Still, he did find you, so we cannot judge him too harshly.' Sarah suspected it would be difficult for Marwa ever to judge Will harshly.

'Who lives out there?' asked Sarah.

Will spoke up. 'I have crossed the desert lands. There are few people left there. The Godawa tribe is all that remains of the southern people, and they are nomads, travelling between the water places. They have adapted and, although they are still allies, they don't want any trouble with Sarin. Tor is their leader.'

'Isn't Tor the one who gave Sarin the scouts to find the water?' asked Sarah.

'To protect their own precious reservoirs, yes,' said Marwa. 'In the meantime, the Godawa people do not get involved in our troubles.'

'They don't sound like allies to me,' sniffed Sarah.

Marwa smiled. 'These are complicated times, Sareka. We, too, have an agreement with Tor, but it is not known abroad. He helps as he can, and buys time for his people.'

Something Marwa had said earlier nagged at the back of Sarah's mind.

'What do these dry wraiths look like?' she asked.

'They are bones shrouded in foul smoke,' said Marwa.

Sarah thought harder, and then she recalled what was troubling her. 'Are they like clouds?' she asked.

'Why?' asked Marwa, his face suddenly grim. 'Have you seen something?'

'I'm not sure,' said Sarah, 'It's just that before I entered the cavern for the first time, I thought I saw clouds on the top of the cliff, except the sky was clear everywhere else, and when I looked again, they were gone.'

'Anwar preserve us! That was almost a moon ago!' cried Marwa, and for the first time Sarah saw fear in his eyes. 'Are you quite sure, Sareka?'

'No,' answered Sarah, 'I only thought I saw something.'

'We can't take any chances,' said Marwa gravely. 'If it was a dry wraith, it's had time to report back to its master. You must leave at once.'

'What, tonight?' asked Sarah, and she realised she was suddenly afraid, very afraid. 'But I'm not ready,' she cried. 'Surely, Marwa …' Her voice trailed off.

'The only thing we can be sure of is if Sarin knows you are in Hutanya, he will have sent out his creatures to try to prevent you from ever leaving Karst, let alone approaching the Teeth.' The sorcerer's voice rang out and filled the cave. 'Archana, Calum, tell the batlings to prepare to carry the message to the south and the High Plains! Make haste! The final battle begins!'

The cavern echoed with Marwa's command, and in the stillness that followed, Sarah heard the whirring of a thousand wings. A sea of black batlings swirled above them. Instinctively, Sarah covered her head and then she heard the call within, primeval and wild, a battle cry which enveloped her and brought her to her feet, her arms spread wide, her long hair streaming out around her. *'It has come to this. I have returned. So be it.'* The words echoed in her mind.

She opened her eyes. Within the fluttering of many wings, she saw a tunnel, grey sky and the high peaks of mountains. She saw herself standing before a tall, menacing shape. She felt a deep, unendurable hurt pierce her heart. Something fell, and she called out, and called out again. The vision faded.

She felt Marwa's hands, gentle on her shoulders. He turned her slowly towards him. His face reflected her emptiness. 'Sareka,' he said quietly. 'Sareka, can you hear me?'

Sareka. Yes, that is who I am ... Sarah struggled with the voice inside her head. *I am awakening*, she thought. *It's true I have been here before, but I can't really remember anything clearly …*

Let it come slowly. Marwa's mouth wasn't moving, but his voice reached inside her. *Let us speak so. It is easier if the boy does not hear.* Marwa glanced at Will, who was watching the circling batlings above.

Sarah realised she was hearing Marwa's thoughts and that he could also hear hers.

I was calling, thought Sarah. *I gave voice to the cry. I, Sareka.*

Yes, Sareka, you are coming back to us … Marwa's eyes sparkled.

How much time has passed? she asked, her mind probing forward to hear Marwa's unspoken reply.

Perhaps too much, Sareka.

Sarah felt her heart fill with aching. She glimpsed a memory of tangled green forests, dancing with light, filled with laughter and bird calls mingling with a boy's voice, crooning her to sleep in a hammock of soft grasses.

Sareka, the voice whispered, *Sareka, sweet dreams.* Whose voice she didn't know, but it didn't seem so important. To recognise that it was a voice she knew was enough, for now. She had begun to remember.

SIX

'Sareka?' Will's face was a nose from hers. His breath was warm and smelled of cinnamon. From somewhere deep in the caverns, she heard the rustling of many batlings' wings. Sarah blinked, and the small face before her lit up with a smile, like a candle in the dark.

'You've been sleeping since yesterday and you haven't even moved for hours,' the boy said reproachfully, and then he glanced guiltily over his shoulder. 'Marwa said I was not to disturb you.'

'I'm here,' she whispered. *And not here*, Sarah added silently. The awakening the previous day had not been complete. She understood this. She was still Sarah, but an older intelligence had sprung alive inside her. Like an ember that feeds on a sudden gust of wind, the pattern of a greater knowledge and old arts danced in her mind. *I have been here*, it told her, *and I know things*.

The new feelings were not strange, but like old friends, loved and welcome, appearing unexpectedly on the doorstep of her memory. She had spent the day in a dream state, between sleep and meditation, gathering wisps of memories together.

'Are we leaving?' she asked Will.

The small boy sat back on his heels. 'Marwa says that depends on you.'

Sarah saw Calum hovering above them. 'Marwa asked me to attend you until you awoke, and to find out how you are feeling, Lady,' the batling said.

Will started to answer, but Sarah forestalled him. 'Tell him …' she began, and then she hesitated, but only for an instant. 'Tell him we are ready to begin our quest.'

Calum's ears twitched and a low growl curled in his throat. He rose and circled gracefully above her, his brown coat gleaming with gold. He dipped his wings once, and grazed the wall of the cavern, casting his gilded glow on the forest mural like a shooting star. He lit the scene so realistically that Sarah could have sworn she saw the towering trees tremble in a tropical breeze, and heard insects singing before the rains. Then he was gone, flitting through the throat of the passage beyond and swallowed by the darkness.

Will sat beside her in silence, but she could feel the excitement quivering through him. They did not speak, but their eyes met and Sarah smiled wanly. He reached up and took her hand.

Soon Marwa's tall shadow preceded the sorcerer into the cavern. When she saw him, Sarah caught her breath. A light flickered in the fierce blue gaze that had not been there before. And then Sarah recognised it, the same light she remembered seeing, from earliest memories, in her parents' eyes, clapping as they sang, 'Happy Birthday'. Which party it was she couldn't remember, but she was wearing a pink dress and Aunt Jenny had on a silly hat and was blowing up a balloon. She could see her mother and father standing together and holding their breath as she blew out the candles on her cake. She remembered their eyes. Marwa's eyes held the same light as he came towards her.

He loves me, she thought, *and I knew him well some time in the past. I love him, too. He is my family here, perhaps all I ever had in Hutanya …*

Marwa placed his palms gently on her cheeks and looked intently at her. This time Sarah was not mistaken. Tears glistened in his eyes. There was a long silence and then his craggy face slowly softened to a smile.

'Is it true? Do you begin to remember?' he asked quietly.

Sarah nodded.

'So,' Marwa said, drawing her into the circle of his embrace. 'Sareka, you are well come. Welcome home.'

They talked long into the night. Marwa asked Sarah many questions but she could give him few answers. He listened to her scattered memories and filled in some of the gaps, but Sarah sensed there were things he did not tell her, harsher memories which he kept from her.

'As I told you before, after you went south, we lost you,' the old man said quietly. 'You simply disappeared.'

'And how old was I when I went to meet Sarin?'

'As Sareka, you were twelve years old, but mature beyond your years. You were coming full into your powers. You knew Sarin better than …'

But Sarah interrupted the wizard, 'Wait! My twelfth birthday was when I came through the door. Time is so different here. How can I have been twelve, twelve years ago?'

'I don't know myself,' admitted Marwa. 'Perhaps it is some trick of time between our worlds, or your worlds, I should say. Sarah's and Sareka's worlds.' He paused. 'What can you tell me about your meeting with Sarin?' he asked quietly.

Much of what Sarah remembered was fragmented and came to her in scattered images. 'I know the waters were drying up,' she said. 'I was here. I have memories of Hutanya's forest. But I don't remember going south.' Sarah closed her eyes, trying to will some sort of recollection to come. She shook her head in despair.

Marwa consoled her. 'Your awakening is incomplete,' he explained. 'Calm yourself. I am grateful for the beginning.' He patted her hand, and Sarah felt his own tremble.

'There isn't much time, is there?' she said.

Marwa did not meet her eyes. 'You must rest, my child. You have not the strength now, after this sudden knowing, to make a journey of this magnitude.'

'Marwa, if there isn't time …' Sarah caught her breath as a picture sprang to her mind. She was a small child, swinging on a tree limb low to the ground, her silver hair wreathed with white flowers, their scent delicate and clinging. Marwa was there, looking not so much younger, but strong, the strongest man in the world as he towered over her, his face lit with a benevolent smile as he waggled the tree limb, springing her high in the air. A bright red parrot sat on his shoulder, cocking its head at her as she arced above the ground.

The vision faded, and they sat in silence.

'Do we still have a chance?' Sarah asked finally.

Marwa's eyes met hers, shifted to Will and then back again.

'I don't know,' he said quietly.

Beside her, Sarah heard Will gasp.

'Then,' she said, rising from the cushions, 'we must leave at once.'

A light spray of water misted her skin as Will leapt to her side. 'Yes!' he cried, and they looked at Marwa. The old man gazed at them with concern and Sarah was suddenly reminded of the odd sense of loss she had felt in the kitchen when she had sat on her father's lap and realised she was growing up.

Marwa drew in a deep breath. 'So be it,' he said. 'We must try.'

'Then we may leave, Marwa?' Will asked.

'At once,' replied the old man. 'You must leave at once.'

Their departure was a blur to Sarah. Later she recalled with amazement the speed of their preparations. Marwa issued many final instructions, batlings flurried about, rucksacks were produced, and they were led through the labyrinth of the cave to an exit. When they first stepped out into the open air, Sarah had to quell an urge to cry out. It was bracingly cold, and the sky above her was studded with spangled light.

'There is Grona, the Wanderer,' said Marwa, pointing to a red star overhead. 'Follow her west. Keep the Sisters,' he continued, pointing to a bright constellation, 'on your left for this night's journey. After that follow ...'

'Arden,' finished Sarah. 'Follow Arden north to the High Plains before the Teeth.'

Marwa beamed at her like a proud uncle. 'Yes, follow Arden.' He looked at her closely, gently grasping her shoulders. 'You have been to the High Plains many times, Sareka. How much of the way do you remember?'

Sarah paused before answering. Into her mind flew a vision of tall blue grass, laid low by sweeping winds, and a jagged outline of cruel peaks in the distance. 'I can see parts of the way, like pieces of a puzzle,' she said, 'but I can't be sure of anything. There's so much missing.'

Marwa patted her shoulders. 'The knowledge is only sleeping. Do not force it to come too quickly.'

They both turned at a scuffling noise beside them. Will was struggling to shoulder his rucksack, his small form dwarfed by its bulk. His face was alight with anticipation of the adventures ahead.

'Guard each other well,' Marwa said. He reached down and pulled a recalcitrant strap over Will's small shoulder. 'So,' Marwa addressed the boy, 'you begin the quest. Remember what I have taught you.' His voice was gruff but his eyes bespoke his deep affection for the child.

'I won't forget, Marwa,' said Will, his face grave. Then he flung himself at the old man and they clung together.

Marwa gently drew back and knelt down to face Will.

'I know you wish to make me proud,' he said softly. 'But please, take care. *San bu kanca na bie*,' he added, raising his hand in salute.

Will raised his hand and responded, '*San ku kana na lie.*'

Their words were strange to Sarah, and yet she understood that a blessing had been exchanged between the boy and the old man.

Calum and Archana whirled overhead, and Marwa raised his hand in farewell. Then he lifted his great head and gave voice to one sharp, haunting cry, a belling that echoed against the high cliffs and soared into the night.

'That should keep them for a while,' he growled and then the travellers walked out into the vast expanse of desert.

SEVEN

Sarah felt small and exposed under the canopy of stars. Although she knew Sarin and his wraiths were far to the north, the destruction of their passing was all around her. There was no evidence that this land had once been a vast rainforest. Before them stretched a barren desert, its emptiness broken only by scattered boulders.

Her rucksack was surprisingly light for its size. Will told her that its fabric had been spun by a kind of caterpillar that had once lived in the great forests of long ago. Marwa had given her a skirt of the same material for their journey. In the old days of Hutanya, the people had even covered their longboats with the stuff, for it was both waterproof and buoyant. There was not much use for either of those qualities now, thought Sarah ruefully.

In spite of her earlier fears, she felt exhilarated to be out in the air, and would forget, for increasing stretches of time, the serious nature of their journey, losing herself in the soft scrunch of sand beneath her feet, the bright night sky spilling above them. Once she almost screamed when a flicker leapt ahead of her, until she realised it was Ashrok, the lizard, who had joined them somewhere along the way.

As soon as Sarah and Will had left Marwa at the caves, Calum and Archana had flown on ahead to serve as scouts. Will was quiet beside her. She could sense his excitement, and at the same time she felt a vibration of intense concentration emanating from him, as though he was listening for something. She did not disturb him with conversation. She tried to focus on the task at hand, to cross the desert to the High Plains as quickly as possible. She tried not to think about Sareka, her other self, following Marwa's instruction to let the knowledge awaken in her in its own time.

She studied the landscape, the occasional cliffs which loomed and faded off to their left as they travelled north. As the night waned, the dunes became mounds, and by the time the stars whispered out and the first grey light appeared in the east, they found a small outcrop of rocks in which to rest. Sarah and Will laid out their sleeping robes, munched on dried roots from their provisions, their eyes drooping with fatigue, and fell into a deep, unconscious sleep.

Sarah awoke, feeling greatly refreshed, just as the sun slipped beyond the horizon. She sat up and looked around their campsite. The silence of the flat, dry land made her feel very small and alone.

But she wasn't alone. Beside her Will stirred and opened his eyes, surveying the land around them. 'It's so beautiful!' he said. He crawled out of his sleeping robes and stretched.

'You mean the desert?' Sarah asked.

The boy spread his arms wide and spun in a circle. 'Yes, and just being outside! It's so … so … I don't know, so full of different colours from the caves.'

Sarah looked out at the bleak landscape. She didn't see much colour in the dim light. To the east were the hulks of high grey dunes. To the north, a steady rising of the desert floor gave way to distant blues, perhaps the beginning of the High Plains. It looked so far away!

She turned to the task of rolling up their robes, and Will sprang to help her, spraying his mist directly into her eyes. As she glanced up, Sarah saw a glimpse of the colours of which Will had spoken. The sky blushed deep plum and peach, and the dunes were the colour of smoky pearls. The distant plains shimmered like fields of sapphire. Then Sarah blinked, and the land returned to its dull, neutral tones.

'My goodness, Will,' she cried, 'you move in a prism!'

'What's that?' asked Will, interrupting his bouncing about to satisfy his boundless curiosity.

Sarah remembered Aunt Jenny holding up a long crystal to the sunlight in her bedroom. How had she explained it? 'It's a shape that bends light and makes colours,' she replied, and hoped she wouldn't be pressed for a further explanation. 'We must eat and move on,' she said, briskly. 'Marwa said there's little time.'

Obediently, Will rummaged through the pack carrying their provisions. He laughed in delight, drawing out a sack of grasses.

'Look, Sareka,' he said, 'Marwa sent yuck!'

After a breakfast of herb water, chevis and bread, they set out, the light almost gone, except for lingering shadows. Sarah wondered at the energy she felt. When she mentioned it to Will, he was silent for a little while, and then said, 'I've been thinking about that. I believe it was Marwa's gift.'

'Marwa's gift?' Sarah stopped and peered at him.

'Every traveller receives a gift. Sometimes it is water, easily found at every stop. Sometimes it is the ability to track. For us, I think Marwa chose sleep.'

Sarah thought a moment and then said, 'I don't mean to sound ungrateful, but wouldn't another gift have proved more useful? We would sleep in any event. The idea of finding water easily sounds a lot more practical.'

Will grinned and shrugged his shoulders. 'Marwa had a reason, I'm sure, to think sleep would be best. And besides, don't you feel wonderful?'

Sarah had to agree. As she opened her mouth to say as much, Will suddenly bolted ahead, calling over his shoulder, 'Race you to the boulders!'

There was a flicker in the sand as the lizard, Ashrok, appearing from nowhere, joined in the contest.

'That's not fair!' Sarah laughed in protest as she leapt into action behind them. 'Hey!' she called into the night. 'Wait for me!'

The journey was much the same that night and for the next few nights to follow. The high plateau appeared only slightly closer before disappearing altogether as their way fell into a huge shallow valley. Sarah and Will walked as briskly as possible through the long desert nights, made their camp before dawn and woke as twilight descended to take up their journey again.

On the sixth evening of their journey, they woke to a new fragrance in the air.

'We must be approaching the High Plains!' cried Sarah.

'I think you're right,' said Will. 'I can smell something delicious, Sareka. What is it?'

Sarah drew a deep breath. A faint sweet perfume drifted down from the rising land to the north. 'I think it's flowers!' she told Will.

'What are flowers?' he asked. 'No, don't tell me, I'll see them soon enough. I've never been to the High Plains, you know.'

Sarah prepared a light meal to carry them through the first part of the night's walking. She was startled to find a bee sharing her herb tea, its tiny tongue darting into the sweet liquid.

'Is that a flower?' asked Will.

'No,' Sarah laughed. 'A flower is … well …'

Will interrupted her. 'Do you remember the High Plains, Sareka?'

Sarah sipped her tea and let her mind open, as Marwa had taught her. *Blues and greens, and a soft surging sound. Laughter, and oh such happiness … someone holding her hand, dark eyes …*

The vision faded abruptly. Sarah almost cried out in disappointment. She became aware that Will was still waiting for her answer.

'We will be happy there, I think,' she said.

Archana and Calum had flown ahead as soon as the light had begun to fade, but Sarah saw that there were other creatures besides the bats and bees flitting above them in the dusky sky.

'What are *those*?' she asked Will.

'Cardamas!' said Will, and he whirled off after a dark winged shadow. He returned with a mottled brown moth, twice the size of his fist, resting on his extended finger. 'Don't be afraid,' he coaxed, as Sarah approached shyly. 'Take it.'

Sarah raised a finger, and the cardama obligingly hopped onto her hand. It was like a giant moth, except for its large eyes, which gazed curiously back at Sarah.

The cardama fluttered her long lashes and spoke. 'Greetings, Lady.'

Sarah blinked and the cardama blinked back.

'Forgive me,' said the cardama, 'I am Shanila. Perhaps you don't remember me?'

Sarah cleared her throat to cover her surprise at being addressed by the cardama. She would have to get used to talking to animals. She looked closely at Shanila and shook her head regretfully. 'I'm sorry,' she said. 'I don't remember.'

The creature flexed her spindly legs, six in all, and lowered her thick lashes. 'It was my pleasure to serve you before. I am here to offer my assistance.'

'Thank you, Your Highness,' Sarah answered. *Your Highness?* she thought. The cardama spread her wings and Sarah gasped at the intricate beauty of their design, a batik fabric of indigo swirls and tiny dots of delicate copper.

Shanila smiled. 'I see you have not forgotten me entirely. But I will refresh your memory. I am queen of night creatures. There are still many of us who have survived the great drought. What we lack in size, we make up for in numbers. When the waters were seized we slept and gathered our strength in the hidden reservoirs of the land.' She fluttered off Sarah's hand and alighted on her shoulder.

'I have come to assist in your awakening, for the cardama are the keepers of legends. I will journey with you on these last nights in the desert, to tell you the old stories and remind you of the powers you possess while you are still awakening to them.'

'But how did you know we were here?' asked Sarah.

Shanila's wings fluttered. 'My dear, you are crossing the desert at night, under cover of darkness. Do not fear that others will discover you. Normally we do not travel across the desert lands. We come from the High Plains, where there is still sweet nectar to be found. Your companions, the batlings, flew ahead to prepare us for your coming. Lady Lia sent me.'

Before Sarah could ask about Lady Lia, she felt a memory stirring.

'Shanila ...' Sarah repeated the name thoughtfully. 'Shanila, Queen of the Shadows Before the Light.'

'Shanila,' repeated the cardama, and bowed her wings gracefully. 'At your service.'

EIGHT

The young man's breath streamed before him. 'Curse this ball,' he hissed. 'I can't get a clear view.' He was speaking to no one, unless you counted the wraiths, wretched miserable shreds of life that they were. The cold penetrated his deep-fleeced robes, woven in an earlier time from the cocoons of cardama. Even after all these years, he couldn't get warm, really warm. It was the single thing he missed about Hutanya. Nothing else.

It was the crystal ball that had given him away to Marwa in the first place. Twelve years ago almost to the day. But he had been not much more than a child then, and he had underestimated the old man's powers of perception.

It didn't matter now. He had what he needed. She was back. And she was coming right to him. With the boy.

He drew a deep breath and concentrated all his attention on the crystal before him. There was only a swirling at first, but slowly an image formed. Two figures travelling under the night sky. And the watcher.

He wished he could see her face, whether she had changed much, besides the ageing. 'Soon enough,' he consoled himself. 'Soon enough I'll see you, just once before the end.'

The image faded, and Sarin saw his own reflection in the shimmering sphere. He cursed in frustration. A wraith who had just entered the chamber cowered and scuttled out again.

'Get back in here, you miserable sack of bones,' growled Sarin.

The wraith slithered back into the room. 'Forgive me, my most powerful Lord, darkest of the dark …'

'Silence, worm!' hissed the sorcerer. 'I have a command.'

The wraith fell at Sarin's feet, grovelling. 'Anything, oh Master of …'

'Silence, I said! Gather my lieutenants in the council chamber. I will meet them there shortly.'

'As you wish, oh great and gifted one!' The wraith scuttled backward out the door, leaving its foul stench hanging unpleasantly in the chill air.

Sarin did not notice. He was gazing once again at the magic crystal. 'Soon,' he whispered, 'I will have all that I desire and more. And she shall lay it at my feet!'

NINE

Many memories returned to Sarah during the following nights as they journeyed across the last of the desert sands. The cardama queen came to them at dusk and stayed until the final hour of the darkness, when they made camp and settled at dawn to sleep. Shanila would perch on Sarah's shoulder and fan her wings softly in the gossamer air, whispering stories and songs from the lost forest and the High Plains and the Godawa lands to the south, tales of camaraderie and festivals, of love and bravery. Throughout their night passage, the cardama queen wove the Old Magic into the telling, spinning the threads of memory for Sareka. It was after the stars dimmed their fiery light and the travellers had settled in their sleeping robes that the dreams would fall upon Sarah. Whole epics of the struggle between the forces of light and darkness would unfold, as she slowly awakened to remembering, in her sleep, to the knowledge and lore of the old ways. There were still paths barred; her own history as Sareka was blocked from her mind. But the land as it once had been rose before her dreaming eyes, an ornate tableau of people and creatures, all the vibrant life of lost Hutanya.

Above all rose the towering trees, their canopies spread like floral skirts before the sun and rain, their dark undersides a delight of coolness and shade. To their lower branches clung slow furry beasts with wide eyes and nimble toes, their young clutching their backs and breasts. Great cats lounged in the forked limbs with coats that shimmered gold and green. On the forest floor, huge boars with magnificent tusks ranged, and mice-like creatures with impossibly long tails scuttled from their paths. These were the memories of Sareka, but Sarah knew them well. They were preserved in the murals of the caverns where she dwelt with Marwa and Will in those weeks before the journey began.

Then came the night, after Shanila had spun her enchanted tales like a fine tapestry around them, when the cardama told them it would be her last visit.

'Soon you will reach the High Plains. Time is running fast and we all have our duties to perform. Rein will meet you there.'

At the mention of the Dasai leader's name, Sarah felt a stirring anticipation. Rein had featured often in the stories of Shanila; his wisdom and bravery were legendary. She was looking forward to meeting him — very much indeed.

She felt the need to hurry for other reasons as well. She was restless in her sleep, and while the dreams delighted and renewed her, in the late hours of her slumber, Sarah sensed a shadow, heavy and foreboding, like a storm in the distance, moving towards them.

Will was causing her worry as well. During the nightly treks, he would listen with shining eyes to Shanila, his skin glowing with light and dew. But he seemed smaller and pale, as though he was being physically drained by the adventure. His appetite was as voracious as ever, and he still skipped through their night passages, but he was … was changing in ways Sarah found difficult to accept. He appeared to be growing younger.

After Shanila bade them farewell, they chose an outcrop of rocks that formed a rough ring for their day's sleep. Sarah smiled to herself as Will laid out their sleeping robes, plumped their pillows and then sat back on his heels to survey his work with satisfaction. He caught her smiling eyes and beamed back at her. A fierce love for him seized her, and she vowed silently that, no matter what, she would protect the boy from the dangers that lay ahead.

'What are you thinking, Sareka?' Will asked.

'Oh, nothing much,' Sarah murmured.

They nestled into their sleeping robes. Sarah saw that Ashrok had curled up into a small ball beside Will's ear. She had hardly seen the lizard in the past days, and assumed he rode inside Will's backpack most of the time. She shuddered at the thought of touching the lizard, and hoped he had no interest in her own pillow. As if reading her thoughts, the lizard rolled open its outer eyelids and glared at her with yellow eyes.

He doesn't like me much either, she thought, as she shifted away from Will to avoid the lizard's malevolent stare. As she was pondering this realisation, the sky began to lighten and Marwa's gift overtook her.

TEN

The day had already faded well into dusk when Sarah woke up. Her sleep had been dreamless, and she felt as though she were rising to consciousness from the depths of a dark sea. She glanced hurriedly around, found Will's small bundle of sleeping robes and knelt beside him. His rosebud lips were parted, his arms flung over his head. The lizard was nowhere in sight. For a heart-stopping moment, she thought Will was too still, until she saw the slow rise and fall of his chest. He looked so innocent, she regretted having to wake him, but Shanila had told them the grasslands lay one night's journey to the north, and the Arden star had already begun its climb in the sky.

'Will,' she whispered, and then froze. Something had shifted behind one of the rocks. There was little light, but she was sure of it. The shadow she had felt moving ever closer was here.

'Will!' she hissed urgently, and his eyes flew open and found hers. 'Shhh,' she whispered, more gently, trying to calm her thundering heart, and she gestured towards the rocks.

'Wraiths?' he whispered back, and she knew then that it was indeed wraiths, the cloud servants of Sarin.

'What should we do?' Sarah asked.

Will chewed his lower lip thoughtfully, still gazing up at her, and in spite of her fear, Sarah felt a lifting of her spirit at the sight of his small perfect face.

'Think,' he replied. 'Think, Sareka. It will come to you.'

A shadow flitted to her left, and Sarah whirled towards it. Nothing was there.

'I can smell them,' said Will, wrinkling his nose. 'They stink of old bones.' He struggled up from under the blankets and peered into the darkness.

This time they both saw it, a wavering whiteness just beyond the ring of stones. Sarah felt a surge of anger welling above her shivering fear. She rose up suddenly and took a step forward.

'What do you want?' she called, and her voice rang like a bell tongue struck against the stones. The dim figure reappeared, closer this time, but still beyond the wall of towering stones.

'Go back,' came a thin reedy voice. 'Go back and leave the boy. We will not follow.'

Leave the boy? Never! thought Sarah, and she drew Will close to her.

'We will not go back,' she called out, sounding much braver than she felt. And then she added, 'You go back. Go back to your dark master and tell him I am coming. We will not go back!'

The figure receded behind the rocks and now the travellers saw that there were three, maybe four, of the shadowy figures hovering behind the dark stones.

'We will not let you pass,' the voice replied, but Sarah sensed the wraith lacked conviction.

'You don't have the power to stop us!' she cried defiantly, and prayed she was right. 'We will pass.'

'They can't enter the ring,' Will whispered, pointing to the standing stones. 'This place is of the Old Magic. They have little power here, so far from their lord.'

Sarah gained courage from his words. 'You go back!' she demanded again.

A high, shrieking laugh burst from the shadows, and Sarah felt the hair on the back of her neck tingling. 'Go back?' said the wraith. 'And what will you do if we don't?'

Will's upturned face swam before her eyes. She cast about frantically in her mind for a reply. Then she remembered Marwa's words. *Let it come to you. Do not force the gift.* She closed her eyes, willing herself to be still, and gradually found an oasis of calm within. She sensed the wraiths moving closer, taking her silence for acceptance of defeat, but she forced herself to centre on the quiet knowing that was somewhere in her memory. She felt Will flinch beside her as a shadow fell over them. Then she opened her eyes and stared into the dull silver eyes of a deathhead.

The wraith was leaning over the rock ledge, its long teeth parted in a ghostly grimace. Without thinking, Sarah opened her mouth and sang, *'Al imba sala mi tri umplatio!*' She was speaking in the Old Tongue, the language of magic! The words tumbled out and she gasped at the power that surged through her body at their utterance. The face of the wraith was contorted in a grimace of pain. '*Sayu kai be ata!*' she sang. The words came without calling, a high, clear, melodic chant. She stepped forward, and the hideous creature recoiled, hissing.

A whimper parted its twisted lips. 'Go back … leave the boy …'

'*Hai ama imbrata!*' she sang, and the wraith writhed piteously against the rocks, shifting shape and size. It was smaller now, more head than body. Sarah knew it was weakened, but not yet defeated. She closed her eyes momentarily to strengthen her concentration. She felt the wraith struggle to regain its ebbing power as soon as her eyes broke contact with it.

When she opened her eyes again, she saw something sparkle at her feet. She reached down and lifted the pearly object. It was a shell, a perfect tiny trumpet.

When Will saw what Sarah held before her, he whooped and leapt to his feet. 'Kalu!' he cried. As he uttered the word, the wraith shrieked and withered, dispersing chalky dust as it tried to flee.

'Kalu!' Will cried again, 'Blow into it, Sareka!' Sarah obeyed blindly, raising the shell to her lips. A note of solemn beauty trumpeted against the stones and echoed in the chill desert air. The wraith crumbled into nothingness. The others were nowhere in sight.

'That was wonderful, Sareka!' Will crowed as he danced close to the stones.

'Careful, Will,' Sarah warned. 'We can't be sure they're gone.'

'Oh, they're gone, all right,' said Will, and before she could stop him, he disappeared behind the high wall of stone pillars.

'Will!' cried Sarah. 'Wait, Will!' She grabbed a short stick from the ground and followed him.

When she rounded the stones, Sarah could see no one in the dusky gloom. The evening stars shone faintly, and the last of the desert stretched ahead to the not so distant shelf of the plateau. She stood still, listening. Something cool brushed against her arm and she jumped, waving the stick wildly above her head.

Will's laughter burst out beside her, and she made out his small form against one of the towering stones.

'What's so funny?' she demanded.

Will stepped out of the shadows, still shaking with mirth. 'You are!' he gasped. 'I mean, I'm sorry, but you look so … so fierce!'

Sarah lowered the stick. 'Will, you frightened me!' she said.

Will tried and failed to stifle another gale of laughter. 'I'm sorry,' he choked. 'It's just … after you challenged those horrid wraiths, how could I frighten you?' He crumpled to the ground, holding his sides. 'Oh, Sareka! You are so funny!'

Sarah brushed back her tangled hair. She saw herself as she must have appeared to Will, wild-eyed and brandishing the stick. She sank down beside him and they sat together laughing as Arden rose in the east.

As the stars blinked awake above them, Sarah drew the shell out of her pocket. 'What exactly is this?' she asked Will.

Will cupped his hands and asked, 'May I hold it?' Sarah gently spilled the shell into his palms and it sent off a glitter of sparks as it fell.

'Oh!' Sarah whispered in awe.

'It's a kalu,' said Will. 'A messenger shell. They are rare now, but once Marwa said they travelled farther than any other beings in Hutanya.'

'Beings?' Sarah echoed, and peered into the hollow of Will's small hands.

Will nodded. 'The kalu are ancient. Their spirits preserve a bit of the Old Magic in Hutanya. But they disappeared with the waters. 'I've only seen one other of these before,' he admitted to Sarah. 'Marwa had one, but he sent it to Tor of the Godawa. It carried a message coded in the runes. I remember Marwa sang to it in the Old Tongue.' He turned the shell and peered more closely at it.

'See here,' he said, as Sarah bent to follow his pointing finger, 'you can see a rune engraved! This is the same rune it sang when you blew into it, Sareka! But I don't recognise this one. Do you?'

Sarah reclaimed the shell to study the tiny engraving. The kalu trailed its effervescence as she gently turned it in the faint starlight. She caught her breath; she *had* seen the rune before, repeated on the cavern walls to form an arc above the great waterfall. She smiled and felt tears sting her eyes.

'What is it, Sareka?' asked Will anxiously. He returned her smile uncertainly. 'Are you crying? What does the rune say?'

'It's all right, Will. In fact, it's a good omen, I believe,' Sarah said quietly, and she slipped the shell into Will's pocket. 'Keep it safe,' she said. 'The rune says *rainbow*.'

ELEVEN

Sarah and Will broke camp and began what they hoped would be their last night's journey in the desert. The trail had become stony, and they started climbing perceptibly higher almost at once. The breeze stiffened and carried a rushing sound like the faint echo of the sea curling against the shore.

'This is the sound I remember! It's the wind!' said Sarah.

Will smiled up at her, his face alight with anticipation. 'Look, Sareka! My pack is so light, I can almost carry it on one shoulder,' he boasted.

'That's because you've eaten almost everything in it. I'm surprised you haven't got fat!' teased Sarah, poking at Will's belly.

He giggled and scrambled on ahead.

Sarah's smile faded as she watched him. He was getting smaller, she was sure of it. *What is happening?* she wondered to herself.

The lizard, Ashrok, appeared again. As usual, he was right under Sarah's feet, startling her with his sudden scuttling in the sand. Sarah listened as Will chattered to him, and the lizard responded with loud, bass croaks. She could make no sense of the conversation, and she felt uneasy, as always when the lizard was near. She hoped it wasn't apparent to Ashrok or the boy.

The night sky was brilliant, and the stars wheeled above them in the crisp air. The sea sounds grew steadily as they travelled, making good time.

'I think that must be the grasses of the High Plains we hear,' said Will.

'I hope so,' said Sarah. 'I would love to have a good night's rest for a change instead of sleeping all day.' But more than anything, Sarah was really looking forward to meeting Rein. Rein, about whom she had heard such wonderful stories, the brave defender of Hutanya.

Some hours before dawn, there was a familiar whirring sound and the travellers saw Archana and Calum approaching.

'Hullo, dear friends!' cried Will as the batlings alighted on his rucksack and leaned their pointy noses affectionately against either side of his head. He stroked their furry cheeks, and their contented humming became so fervent that Sarah laughed aloud.

'There are no dangers ahead,' Archana reported.

'And we have seen the Dasai on the move,' said Calum. 'They are headed for the boundary that separates the desert from the High Plains.'

The batlings squeaked with concern as Will

related their confrontation with the wraiths. Archana examined the kalu, and her lovely eyes widened with pleasure when Will mentioned the matching runes in Karst. Sarah suspected she was homesick and missing Marwa. The batlings seemed drowsy from their long night's flight. Calum shifted to Sarah's back to ease Will's burden, although Sarah was surprised at how lightly he clung to her rucksack.

Sarah longed to reach the Plains. The sweet, green scent of the grasses had infused the air for some time now, and she was eager to see what they were really like. The perfumed night brought sparks of memory to her, but she had no clear vision of the place they were fast approaching. After the barren wasteland they had traversed she felt a yearning to see something growing.

Will's small form skipped on ahead of her, his head bobbing in animated conversation with Ashrok.

'Archana says we should reach the Plains by dawn. Won't it be lovely, Ashrok? I mean, I've lived in the desert and the caves all my life, and now I'll finally see real grass. I mean waves of grass, that's what Marwa said. Oh, I hope Marwa is all right, I mean now that I'm not there to be his young eyes. That's what he always calls me, you know, Ashrok. I know the batlings will look out for him, but I miss him so, and worry — he's so wonderfully old, you know. I guess he always has been. Old, I mean, don't you think?'

He hopped lightly on the scrabble of rocks

underfoot, leaving a trail of tiny green tendrils in his wake.

Who is Will? Sarah wondered again. *He seems like a fairy child out of a children's story, so free and innocent. What was it that Marwa had called him? A wish waiting to happen.*

Sarah pondered that description as she trudged along the trail. He could make growing things in this bleak land, and water droplets misted his skin. *He's a rainforest child,* she decided, *even though there's no rainforest left.* A vision of Aunt Jenny rose suddenly in her mind, and a wave of sadness struck Sarah. And what would her aunt think of the terrible destruction of Hutanya?

'Oh, Aunt Jenny,' she whispered, 'will I ever see you and Mum and Dad again?'

But the feeling did not last. Over time in this strange land, Sarah Clare's memories were fading, while Sareka's were becoming more and more focused. It was not that Sarah had forgotten her family, it just seemed that they were people she had known and loved a long, long time ago. She felt a sense of mission now, a crusader's spirit. This was her land, although much of it so far was still unfamiliar to her.

Her feelings of connection to Marwa and Will had grown during the days in the caverns and on the trail. *It's funny,* she thought, *how close I feel to the old man now, even though he's not here. It's as though a part of him is travelling with me.* Shanila's stories had been partially responsible; Marwa figured largely in them, the Master of the Forest, guardian of all the people, animals and plants who dwelt there.

Sareka's own role in the past was less familiar to her. She was a sorceress, and she had been raised by Marwa. These things she had been told, but the old wizard had been careful to explain that it would be far less dangerous to let her history as Sareka unfold in her own memory.

Sarah had asked Will about his parents, but he had no recollection of any family but Marwa. 'I have always been with him,' he had replied simply. 'He says I came to him after the waters died. I don't remember Hutanya, except through Marwa's stories and the murals.'

The travellers walked on through the last of the night, and soon even Will grew quiet as their path continued to climb. The footing was tricky, and often small landslides of stone cascaded beneath their feet. Once, when Sarah was again distracted by the lizard appearing suddenly beside her, she slipped and fell, scraping her knees and the palms of her hands. The batlings hummed about her in concern, and Will, despite Sarah's protests, insisted they stop immediately so that he could cleanse her wounds and apply his herbs.

'They're only scratches,' Sarah said. 'It's nothing, really.' But she allowed him to rub the moist leaves he had drawn from his pack on the small cuts, and she admitted that they were instantly soothed. She smiled fondly as Will went about his doctoring, his face intent and serious.

'This is ancient medicine,' he explained, as he dabbed at her tender skin, 'from the forest of long ago. All our healing was easy then, Marwa says. Now all the forests are gone, and with them, so many wonderful healing plants. Marwa taught me to preserve the old lore of natural medicines, but we have so few of the ingredients left.'

Sarah thought of her Aunt Jenny as she felt the leaves cooling her skin. She had never paid much attention when her aunt spoke passionately about the need to preserve the rainforest. Now she could see a terrible future for her world, and she was beginning to understand why her aunt got so angry at people's unwillingness to change bad habits to preserve the earth's resources.

She broke off her musing as Ashrok scurried around in the litter of stones at their feet and presented Will with a root that he held between his teeth. Will studied it and leapt up in excitement. 'Oh! Thank you, Ashrok. This is a fine gift!' He bit off a piece and extended the other half to Sarah.

'Chew this, Sareka,' he said.

Sarah eyed the brown stick suspiciously. 'What is it?' she asked.

'Go on, try it!'

Reluctantly Sarah popped a bit of the stuff into her mouth. A rich, sweet spearmint flavour burst from the root and she munched happily until it became sticky. 'It's gum!' she cried with pleasure and blew a big bubble.

Will clapped his hands in delight. He demanded Sarah produce another and then solemnly tried to blow his own. A bubble emerged and grew to the size of his small head.

'Be careful, Will,' Sarah warned, but too late. The bubble popped and clung to Will's nose and chin. Undaunted, he peeled it off and tried again.

'We must keep moving,' advised Calum, as he swooped down from above. 'The Dasai are preparing for us at dawn.'

So off they went, their passage punctuated by snaps and pops as Will perfected his new skill.

The night drew on. The constellations crept along on their own parade. Sarah concentrated on the trail which wound steadily upward. Her senses had been honed to night sounds, and she was lulled by the rushing melody of the grasslands ahead. The batlings' presence comforted her. After a brief period of rest, they had stayed with the travellers through the climb, gliding reassuringly above them. There were no signs of the wraiths that had beset them at the ring of stones the evening before.

At last the sky was growing light. Ahead of them,

suddenly appearing in the gloom, Sarah saw a ridge, beyond which there was no higher ground. Her spirit was buoyant, and Will caught her mood and moved closer to smile up at her in shared anticipation.

'Archana,' the boy called softly. 'Archana, what do you see?' The batling dropped down and rested on Will's pack, fanning her wings to keep her weight from straining the tired child.

'Ah,' she crooned, 'Will, this I may not tell you. For this is a sight you must behold with your own eyes. Just ahead, Will. Just ahead lie the High Plains.'

The wind surged and Archana flung herself aloft, as the night surrendered to the dawn. Sarah clasped Will's hand, and they hurried forward until they were just below the last overhang of rock.

Abruptly, Sarah dropped his hand.

'Race for the top!' she sang out, and they were off, leaping over the last boulders that littered the trail. On hands and knees, they grappled over the lip of the ridge, and swung to the top together. The wind rushed over them in a rolling wave of sound, and the sun burst full upon them.

TWELVE

Marwa stirred the fire, as the ashes quickened and died in grey circles and pentagons. Tiny dragons of smoke flickered wispy tongues and streamed upward, disappearing in the darkness of the cavern. He stared into the flames intently, relying on his inner eye to reveal to him what his dulled vision could not. He waited for the sign.

Since the children left, his dreams had been disturbing. He trusted Sareka to guard Will and herself, but he could not deny his fear that the girl would be extremely vulnerable in her confused state. His sleep the previous night had brought a vision of conflict, of wraiths descending on the travellers, and he had been startled awake by a song of the Old Magic. If he hadn't known better, he would have sworn he had heard kalu calling in the Old Tongue.

Whatever it was, the kalu's voice had brought him some comfort, and now he was preparing the fire that would burn until Sareka's quest was completed. He had laid it on the night of the children's abrupt departure, and his visions now prompted him to draw it to life. It would be ready when the time came. He could do no more, and to feel impotent any longer would drive the wizard close to despair. He had to believe the girl would succeed.

In his mind's eye, he could sense their presence now on the cusp of the High Plains. One third of the journey was already completed, and only the grasslands and the Teeth lay between Sareka and Sarin.

And Will.

A surge of dread clutched at his heart at the thought of the beloved boy. He knew Will was at risk, and it had taken all of Marwa's self-control to keep himself from begging the boy to stay with him. But the wizard knew the runes, and he knew that it was Will's right and destiny to accompany Sareka on the quest.

Marwa had not completed the reading when the children were with him. He had not told them that he did not need to see the runes. He knew each line engraved on the murals. He turned now to the great paintings before him, aglow in the firelight. The runes appeared as blurry scribbles to his clouded eyes, but he recited them from memory.

'And it shall be she who comes from beyond the green door who will strike the desert back and set the waters free. And it shall be he who finds her who will accompany her to the chosen ground, though perilous be every step ...'

Marwa broke off, unwilling to continue. 'I will not dwell on a disaster that may not occur,' he muttered aloud. But he knew there would be loss either way, whether Sareka completed her quest or not.

The old wizard turned back to the fire, and continued his careful shifting of the precious logs. He would tend the flames until he saw the sign.

THIRTEEN

Sarah and Will stood motionless on the edge of the High Plains. Before them, as far as the eye could see, swept the tall grasses. The high winds wove intricate patterns and ripples, continuously changing the fabric of the land. There were birds, huge flocks of them, in every colour of brown and green, rising and falling in waves above the tide of blue-green fronds.

The land seemed vast and empty, an endless sea of grass, and then in an instant, a blink of their eyes, the Dasai appeared. A multitude of people and tall beasts erupted from the grasses in a stately procession. Banners of gold and green billowed from tall standards and, above the wind, the sound of drums and cymbals blared. The Dasai approached, golden-skinned, tall and slender as the grass, their bright yellow garments buffeting around them like swirling pools. The animals, long-necked and long-legged, stepped forward gracefully.

Sarah felt Will's small hand creep into hers and she clasped it tightly. The advancing horde and the music stopped abruptly. A group of four Dasai detached themselves from the throng of people and animals. Three men and a girl. Sarah scanned their faces, burnished like rare metal, regal and composed.

The tallest man and the girl halted, and the two younger men stepped silently forward, with their hands crossed over their chests. The only sounds were the incessant surf of grasses and the calling of the birds overhead.

When the young men came towards them, Sarah felt a wave of panic. Their faces were void of greeting or emotion, and she wondered fleetingly if she had led Will into a terrible trap. She drew herself up and took a step forward, shielding Will with her body. She looked steadily at the two young men, and raised her hand in greeting, hoping she looked more confident than she felt.

At the gesture, smiles of joy wreathed their faces, and they presented their palms upturned to the sky.

'Welcome, Sareka!' the shorter of the two cried. 'Welcome, Will! Welcome to the High Plains!'

Then music resounded again around them and a great cheer went up. The two young Dasai tribesmen dropped all formality and embraced Sarah and Will in turn.

The greeters introduced themselves, shouting into their ears.

'I am Maren!'

'And I'm Kay! We remember you well. We would be honoured to join your quest, Lady Sareka!'

The cheering crowd erupted again as they were led to the tall man and the girl who waited, their palms upturned to the sky. Sarah was struck by the man's almond-brown eyes, which blazed out at her from a strong, fine-featured face. His jet-black hair hung loose around his shoulders.

'Greetings, Sareka,' said the tall man, and the people grew quiet to hear his words. 'I am Rein of the Dasai. We have long prepared for this day. Forgive us if our welcome overwhelms you. We know you must be tired from your crossing of the desert land. The people of the Dasai have honoured your memory, and will do whatever is possible to help you defeat the powers of Sarin which threaten us all.' He turned and beckoned to the girl who stood silently behind him.

'Come, Lia, and greet the Lady Sareka and Will.'

Lia glided forward, and Sarah was enchanted by her beauty. Her hair was the colour of ripe wheat, woven with wild flowers in tiny braids that streamed out like a halo in the wind. She too was clothed in brilliant yellow, and she drew a tiny bouquet of white blossoms from the folds of her gown. Sarah watched with pleasure as Lia presented the flowers to Will and kissed him solemnly on his forehead.

'Welcome, little friend,' she whispered. Then she turned to Sarah and offered her forehead for Sareka's kiss in return. When Sarah looked up, she was caught in Rein's intense gaze.

Rein turned his palms towards Sarah, and she instinctively touched them lightly with her own. Her hands tingled with a shock of recognition, but true memory evaded her. As their hands joined, the crowd roared its approval. Rein kept hold of one of her hands, guiding her through the tall grasses with Lia and Will in tow.

'We are still a fair distance from our camp,' Rein called to her above the cheers. Before them, two of the tall beasts knelt with their spindly legs tucked beneath them. 'Meta and Ryu are our finest grazels. Please mount and ride in comfort. You must be exhausted after your long journey on foot.'

Will scrambled happily up on Meta's broad back, his face alight with excitement at the prospect of the exotic ride. Sarah mounted Ryu, the other grazel, with as much dignity as she could muster, and wrapped her fingers in the animal's silky mane. Then up they rose on the towering beasts, and headed for the Dasai campsite.

She glanced over at Rein, who rode beside her. The shock of recognition had not subsided. *I know him well*, she thought, and it suddenly seemed very important to remember something, anything, about him. He looked over at her and smiled for the first time, and Sarah felt her heart lurch. His eyes held such warmth, but they were also guarded, as if he were trying not to reveal something. Sarah wanted to speak with him, to hear his voice, but she felt shy and confused.

As if sensing her discomfort, Rein drew his grazel closer to her. 'We have several hours to ride to our settlement. Let your mind be quiet, Sareka, and let Ryu do the work. There will be time for talk later. I must arrange a few things, if you will excuse me?' He smiled gently, and before Sarah could think of a response, he rode forward to join Kay and Maren.

'You really like him, don't you?' piped up Will from her left side. He was grinning across at her from his perch on the grazel he was riding.

Sarah realised she was blushing, and feeling even more confused and furious with herself, she answered rather stiffly. 'Rein seems like a very kind man …'

Will kept grinning and replied, 'He likes you, too. I can tell.'

'Oh, do you think so?' cried Sarah before she could stop herself.

'Think what?' came Rein's voice from her right. Sarah wondered how much of their conversation he had overheard.

'I was just saying …' began Will.

'… how much we like the High Plains,' Sarah blurted out. She flashed a desperate look at Will before continuing. 'I think you are right, Rein. We should let our minds be quiet.'

Will opened his mouth to speak, and then, seeing Sarah's frantic eyes, he simply grinned again and said no more.

They reached the camp at sunset. Will was drowsy, but

glowed with pleasure as he discussed the ride on the grazel with Ashrok. The lizard had managed to make Sarah spill her tea when they first arrived, and seemed to be continually underfoot as she set about making their sleeping robes ready.

It had been a full night and day since they had slept, but Marwa's gift had not visited them. Will was showing signs of fatigue, but Sarah did not feel at all tired.

The Dasai laid their packs around the fire; their animals milled contentedly beyond the glow of the banked flames. Sarah watched as Will devoured a plate of steaming food, and then she tucked him into his bedroll. As he nestled happily in the warm depths of the robes, she was aware of how little space he filled.

'Will,' she said, 'why are you getting smaller?' She wanted to take back her words, but the question came out before she had stopped to think. Will was definitely smaller, and he seemed to be growing younger as well.

The boy's bright eyes smiled up at her, his innocence even more pronounced by the soft grasses framing his head.

'Perhaps for the same reason you are growing older and taller,' he answered.

Sarah crouched over him, stunned by his response. She looked at her hands as they rested on his sleeping robes, at her long fingers. She stood slowly and realised that it was from a greater height than it should be that she surveyed the camp. She had grown tall.

'I can't be so much older,' she whispered. 'I'm not, am I?' But she knew then it was true. She felt older. She wasn't at all the same carefree girl who had wandered aimlessly in the greenhouse. That day now seemed a very long time ago.

'I noticed it after our second night in the desert,' said Will. 'I don't understand either, but I'd guess you're over twenty turnings of the year by now.' Will smiled sleepily and he turned his cheek against the soft grasses.

'But that's impossib…' Sarah stopped as she remembered that here in Hutanya perhaps anything was possible.

'Maybe it's part of Marwa's gift, maybe not,' said Will softly. 'Time is running fast. It appears that for you it is running faster still, and for me it is running backward.' He yawned and slowly closed his eyes.

Sarah watched him as his breathing slowed into a deep, rhythmic sleep. *If it's true that time is running backward for Will,* she thought, *he'll be a baby before the journey's end!* A wave of panic swept over her. *And what do I know about caring for a baby? How can I send him back without me when we get to the Teeth?*

Sarah felt fear grip her, and forced it down. She had discovered when they had been beset by the wraiths at the standing stones that this was easily within her power. The fear gradually subsided as she felt the part of her that was Sareka respond. *If it's true,*

then I must trust that, as Sareka, I'll know, she reasoned.
I'll know what to do.

Sarah gazed for a long time at Will's sleeping
form before she sensed she was not alone. She turned
to see Rein standing patiently behind her.

'I have come to ask for the honour of escorting
you to the pavilion, if you are not too tired,' he said.
'You must eat first, and then sleep. Tomorrow we can
begin to know each other again, and discuss the journey onward. Tonight, there is music and laughter, of
which I fear you have remembered little in this harsh
awakening.' Rein smiled, and Sarah felt a rush of
pleasure. She had been right, when Will asked her what
she remembered about the High Plains. There would
be laughter.

'Come,' the young man said simply, holding out
his strong brown hand. Sarah grasped it tightly, and
looked into his eyes. She saw dark rivers and felt a
touch of Will's coolness in his palm. 'Yes,' Rein murmured, as if reading her thoughts. 'The waters still rise
in some of us on the High Plains. They are buried
deep, but it is only here that the grasses still grow. The
High Plains you knew had lakes, but they are gone
now.'

'What do you know of me since my return?'
Sarah asked him, as he gently pulled her to her feet.

'While you crossed the last of the desert,
Archana and Calum made contact to tell us of your
return and your quest. They told me there was much

you do not remember,' Rein responded quietly, and Sarah noticed that he did not look at her. There was a small silence between them.

'Shall we go?' he said finally, as his eyes met hers and he smiled again. Sarah nodded and smiled shyly back. They walked slowly towards the main fires. The wind lifted their hair from their shoulders, and sang in Sarah's ears like a seashell's song.

She paused and looked back to where Will was sleeping. A grazel, Meta, grazed close beside him.

'Don't worry,' Rein said. 'Meta was like a nurse-maid to me, and my father before me. Grazels have long lives and they are fiercely loyal. No harm can come to the child when she is near.'

The question of her sudden growing loomed in Sarah's mind. 'Rein,' she asked, 'how old was I when we last met?'

The Dasai stopped and stared out over the plain. 'Eleven,' he answered softly, ' and I was just past my thirteenth year. You came with Marwa to witness the Dasaitai rites.'

'What are the Dasaitai rites?' Sarah asked.

Rein still gazed out over the plains, as if he were seeing the past somewhere among the swaying fronds under the moonlight. 'The Dasaitai rites are our ritual passage ceremonies from childhood into manhood and womanhood. Before I could be made the Dasai leader, I had to be a man.'

He turned then and looked at Sarah.

'If you had not disappeared, you would have also celebrated your passage in Karst in the following year when you turned twelve. And then we planned ...'

Rein stopped short, and took Sarah's elbow. He guided her towards the fire's light in the pavilion ahead.

'We planned ...?' Sarah prodded him. 'Please, Rein. I want to remember.'

Rein regarded her solemnly without speaking. Finally he said, 'Sareka, all there is to know will be known to you. No one can force an awakening. Indeed it is a dangerous path, and I would never wish you any harm. As I said before, now it is a time for food, and song and sleep. Will you trust me in this?'

Lively music drifted across the fields. Sarah smiled and felt safe for the first time in days. 'Yes,' she said. 'Yes, I will trust you. Let's go!'

FOURTEEN

Rein led Sarah into a huge pavilion ringed with cushions. As she sank down gratefully in the soft pillows, a
delicious fragrance of spiced food surrounded her. She
felt ravenously hungry. Kay presented her with a plate
heaped high with steaming vegetables and grains
which she devoured contentedly, licking her fingers to
savour the last bite.

Her appetite sated, Sarah surveyed the tented
area. The tribespeople were all enjoying their evening
meal, and laughter filled the air. The wind had dropped
with the setting sun, and soft music tinkled from tiny
bells that decorated the grazels grazing outside the
pavilion. Torches flared everywhere, and Sarah gazed
with wonder at the carnival of brilliant yellow and
green costumes. She felt a bit drab in her brown homespun skirt.

She smiled across at Maren and Kay, who waved
merrily when they caught her eye. Rein sat
quietly beside her, his presence comforting her. She
felt no need to speak, and she sensed that nothing was
expected of her except that she enjoy the festive mood.

A line of dancers approached the entrance of the
pavilion bearing lighted candles on small plates. Young

boys and girls, their golden skin glowing, wove an intricate trail to the gentle music of gongs. Lia was among them, clad in palest green like the underside of a new leaf.

How lovely she is, thought Sarah.

The dancers spun the plates on their upturned palms, ducking in and out of the line as the music quickened. They twirled and leapt, always keeping the plates steady, until they formed a line of arcing light. It reminded Sarah of a field of fireflies on a summer night.

'The cardama are called,' whispered Rein at her elbow, and Sarah gasped with pleasure as she saw a great flock of the giant moth-like creatures, led by Shanila, swirl into the pavilion. They joined the elaborate dance, their powdery wings grazing the flames, sending sparks of colour skyward. The sparks spilled upon the assembled watchers, sprinkling them with a golden glitter.

As the dance slowed into a final spin, Shanila alighted on Lia's shoulder and, adorning each other, they came to sit with Sarah.

'Oh, that was beautiful!' Sarah cried, clapping her hands together. Lia and Shanila lowered their eyelashes in acknowledgment of Sarah's pleasure, and she was struck by a strange resemblance between them.

'We are honoured,' they replied together, and it was as if they spoke with one voice.

Lia smiled as she saw the question in Sarah's eyes. 'We are star-bound,' she explained. 'That's why you can see similarities. On the night I was born, the Lady Shanila attended my mother and gave her gift of grace to me. And we were born under the same star.' The girl raised her slender arm and pointed to a hole in the centre of the tent top. Grona, the Wanderer, shone brightly through.

Sarah wanted to know more about this charming girl who was perhaps only a few years younger than herself. Just as she was about to ask Lia to tell her more about her life, Maren and Kay appeared and made courtly bows to the two young ladies.

'Come dance with us!' cried Kay as lively music filled the pavilion. Before Sarah could protest, Maren had drawn her to the dance floor, with Kay and Lia joining them amid the throng of revellers.

'I don't know how,' she gasped as Maren led her into a line.

'But of course you do, Sareka,' he said, smiling down at her. 'Just follow me.'

Sarah blushed under his kindly gaze, and raised her arms to touch Maren's fingers. The dancers began with a simple step, and Sarah watched Maren's feet. Two steps forward, two steps back, a turn and their fingers touched again. Two steps right, two steps left and turn. They lifted their arms and formed an archway, as dancers at the head of the line swept under and down the promenade. The music was enchanting, and Sarah glowed with pleasure as she successfully followed Maren's steps. She spun around and found she had a new partner. Kay, his friendly smile matching her own, led her through the steps now. Her feet moved lightly as if from long practice and she laughed aloud.

As she approached the head of the line, Kay released her and she whirled into Rein's embrace. He held her as they promenaded gracefully together under the arch of raised arms.

'Your eyes put the candles to shame,' he whispered as they turned, their fingers brushing, and Sarah felt again the spark in Rein's touch. She turned again, hiding her confusion. *I must indeed be growing up*, she thought, as she saw Rein looking at her with open admiration. Suddenly, she longed for a mirror to confirm his words.

Rein threw back his head and laughed. 'Let me be your mirror, Sareka.'

Sarah gasped in horror. 'You *can* read my mind, just like Marwa could!' she cried, and turned away, her face burning.

Rein turned her gently back to face him. 'My apologies, Lady,' he said, as he swept her along in the dance. 'I did not mean to embarrass you. Your awakening is new, and I don't mean to pry into your thoughts. There are a few of us who still communicate with the Old Magic. You have the gift as well.'

Rein's eyes held hers. She opened her mind and listened.

Yes, Sareka. I hear you. The gift of silent voice exists for some of us. Does it frighten you?

Sarah hesitated. 'I don't know,' she said aloud. The pavilion was suddenly overwhelming to her. The music, the laughter, now seemed to be too close after her long nights alone with Will in the desert. Rein seemed to understand this at once, and silently they slipped out of the dance and walked from the pavilion into the star-studded night.

The wind had died down. It murmured in the grasses as countless voices of insects serenaded the night. They walked aimlessly through the tall reeds until Sarah felt a calmness settle upon her.

She turned and touched Rein's arm. 'I'm sorry,' she said, 'it's just that so much is still new, a mystery. My past, my powers … It's so frustrating, this half-knowing. I feel so, so … awkward!'

'Awkward you are not,' replied Rein. 'You danced like the petals spilling from jungle blossoms.' He took her hands and she turned to face him. 'Forgive me,' he said. 'I don't mean to minimise your struggles to awaken. But I am very happy you have come again, and while it is hard for both of us to be patient, it is this great happiness that prevails. I never thought to know this feeling again.' Rein's eyes blazed into hers, and Sarah felt again a rush of pleasure surge through her. Then as before, she felt him draw away, into himself, as he turned to stare out over the grasses.

'We knew each other well, didn't we, Rein?' asked Sarah quietly. 'Before …'

Rein smiled, but his eyes did not meet hers. 'We

were the best of friends. You came often to the High Plans with …'

Abruptly, Rein turned back to the pavilion. 'It is unfortunate,' he said quietly, 'that your awakening is still in progress. You are vulnerable, Sareka, and your quest will require all your powers. I have no wish to distract you with childhood memories.' Rein did not look at her, and his voice held a distance that had not been there moments before.

A wave of frustration seized Sarah. 'But there's so much I don't know! I don't even know what powers I possess!' she cried. Rein turned back to look at her distraught face, but said nothing. 'Marwa thought he would have had time to instruct me,' she continued, 'and then he learned the wraiths had found the caves. I had to leave. Shanila has taught me the history of Hutanya, but I know so little about myself, as Sareka. You knew me.' Sarah gazed up at the familiar sky. She felt small and powerless. 'I know only a part of myself as Sareka, and the part I thought I knew so well, as Sarah, is disappearing. I was a girl from another world who fell through a door. Now I'm growing up faster than I ever wanted to.' The fears Sarah had been afraid to name were tumbling out of her. There was no stopping now. She looked beseechingly at Rein's unfathomable eyes in the darkness. 'I want to help! I'll do anything!' she said vehemently. 'I'm just not sure how.' She drew a deep breath that ended in a sob. 'I'm afraid,' she whispered softly.

For a moment, Rein stood unmoving before her, and then Sarah felt his arms draw her close to him. 'We're all afraid, Sareka,' he said, close to her ear. 'You're not alone.'

'When we were children, we would camp out every night on the plains. You came for the summer months, when the rains poured down in Karst. We used to play a game. We would make wishes and wonder what would happen if they came true.' Rein sat beside Sarah in a circle of waving grasses. They had been talking for hours.

'Like what?' Sarah lay back and gazed up at the stars glittering above.

'We would wish that a giant lizard would come and take us flying across the jungle to Godawaland. Or that a magic boat would take us shooting down the rapids of the Tobin River.' Rein smiled as he turned his face to the sky. There was a short pause before Rein asked. 'What did you wish for, when you were beyond?'

'I used to wish to go swinging on huge trees, vine to vine, and that I could dive into clear green pools and ...' She looked suddenly at Rein. His eyes were bright in the darkness. 'Oh, Rein, do you think I was remembering Hutanya?'

'No, Sareka,' he said, 'I don't *think*. I know.'

'What do you wish for now, Rein?' asked Sarah quietly.

Rein turned and looked down at Sarah as she lay beside him. 'I don't make wishes any more,' he said, and Sarah had the feeling again that he was becoming distant. 'Perhaps if you have everything you want, everything you wish for, you only start to worry about someone or something taking it away from you.' He sighed, and stood in silence.

Sarah rose as well and they stood side by side, listening to the rush of the grasses in the night breeze. 'Look!' she said, pointing to a blazing ball of orange streaming its tail across the sky. 'Was that a comet?' She caught a look of puzzlement on Rein's face, and then he turned away.

'It was the Wanderer's twin,' he answered quietly. 'Grolan.'

Sarah looked up and found the star that had led her across the desert. 'Grona is the Wanderer. She is there. What is the story of her twin, Grolan?'

Rein's gaze drew her eyes to his face.

'What?' she asked.

Rein looked back at the sky and didn't respond for so long that Sarah thought perhaps she hadn't spoken her question aloud. Then she remembered that didn't matter. Rein could read her thoughts.

'The legend is that Grona wanders in search of her twin, who fell from favour with the sky. He is literally falling, and she is trying to catch him.'

'What did Grolan do?' asked Sarah.

Rein took her hand. 'He tampered with the laws of nature. Come now, you are shivering. Let's go back.'

Sarah was surprised to discover that it was true; she was shivering, but she wasn't cold.

FIFTEEN

When Sarah and Rein rejoined the festivities in the pavilion, the entire tribe had risen and the gongs gently intoned a repeated refrain. Then Lia, with the Lady Shanila on her shoulder, stepped into the centre of the tent and began to sing.

Lia's voice was like a fairy's kiss, light and pure. The song was the story of Sareka's quest, as yet incomplete. The green door which had opened onto the desert of Karst, the deep caverns where she had studied with Marwa, and the nights of journeying across the desert to the High Plains were all told in song. Sarah was captivated as the lovely girl sang of her journey.

Lia sang of the desert nights, of Shanila, the cardama queen, of the defeat of the wraiths at the ring of stones. She sang of the Arden star, guiding Sarah and Will through the long nights, and of the greeting of the Dasai and their arrival at the camp.

Impulsively, Sarah stepped forward and took Lia's hand. She joined the younger girl in the chorus of the song and their voices soared in harmony. As she finished, Sarah realised she had been singing the last lines alone. Suddenly shy, she stopped. Her last note shimmered and died in the cool evening like a shooting star. There was silence, and then laughter and clapping as her new friends embraced her. Sarah smiled shyly and put her palms together in acknowledgment of their appreciation. Every gesture she made was familiar. She felt like she belonged here. She felt safe, loved, at home.

Rein stepped forward and took her hand. 'After that performance, we shall abound in dreams of delight,' he said, formally. 'Come, it is late. We will see you are comfortably settled for the night, Lady.'

Sarah nodded, still in a daze from the release of her song. She accepted, finally, after spilling her innermost thoughts to Rein, what was happening to her. She was becoming more Sareka and less Sarah, and she had been fighting it, preventing her own awakening. Now she would put the life of Sarah behind her. It was necessary for her quest, for her survival, for the survival of them all.

Sarah looked up at the stars as they walked slowly through the camp. The tinkling of grazel bells drifted on the air as the grazels knelt to rest, and there was a soft murmur of voices as the Dasai prepared for bed. Nearby, Sarah heard a baby cry and the crooning of its mother soothing the child back to sleep.

Meta snuffled softly in greeting as they approached Sarah's fire, and stretched her neck in pleasure as Rein caressed her long muzzle. Rein offered his hand silently to Sarah, and she felt the tension of unspoken words pass between them as he gently squeezed her fingers and turned to go.

Sarah gazed down at Will's small form curled in a ball beneath the sleeping robes. She sank down beside him and drew her fingers lightly across his cheek. The child smiled, but did not stir. *I will protect him*, she thought, *no matter what happens in the future*.

Shadows flickered between the many fires. Sarah pulled her blankets around her and hugged her knees. She wished on the first star that caught her eye.

'Rain,' she whispered, surprising herself. 'I wish for rain.' And she wondered what it was she really meant.

SIXTEEN

The next morning Sarah woke to bird song. The sun was warm on her face. It felt strange to be waking up in the early daylight. As she opened her eyes, she was greeted by the sight of Will trying to coax Meta, the grazel, to kneel.

'That's it,' he was saying softly, as he waved a handful of chevis in front of the towering grazel's nose. 'Lovely yuck for Meta, and then a ride for Will!'

The grazel accepted the grass and then patiently lowered herself to allow the boy to climb up on her back. Will's face was alight with his triumph, and then he glanced cautiously around from his perch. Sarah closed her eyes, feigning sleep, and peeked out through lowered lids.

Will cleared his throat. 'Up, Meta!' he commanded. 'Up, girl!'

The grazel rose gracefully and Sarah fought to suppress a giggle as she saw Will's eyes widen in alarm at the beast's swift response and his new precarious height.

'Good girl,' the boy said softly. 'Now, let's go ... but not too fast, if that suits you ... Meta?'

The grazel pivoted her head on her long neck to

give Will a long, steady look. She did not move.

'Um, that's if you want to … I mean, go, um … How about a little walk?' The boy's voice trailed off uncertainly as Meta snorted and continued to stand, chewing the chevis. She bent her long neck down and rummaged through Will's knapsack in search of more grass. Ever curious, Will leaned over her neck to watch, and before he could right himself, he was sliding down it onto the ground. He landed with a thump right by Sarah's head.

Sarah's eyes flew open in mock surprise. 'Why, Will,' she drawled sleepily, 'whatever have you been up to?'

Will glanced guilty at Meta and then replied, 'Oh, nothing much. Just, um, feeding Meta.'

'Ummm,' said Sarah, as she sat up and stretched. 'So I see.' There were clumps of grass scattered around their sleeping robes. 'Has she eaten all of our chevis?'

Will sprang up hastily and moved their packs away from the grazel. 'Oh no, Sareka,' he reassured her, 'just a little bit.'

'Too bad,' Sarah murmured, and she stood and began to fold up their belongings. She surveyed the camp around them. The air was pungent with cooking fires, the ever-present breeze carrying the scents of tea and herbs, and the warm, earthy smell of the grazels. The people, dressed in their sunbright clothes, went about their morning activities of cooking and sweeping, calling soft greetings to one another.

A young boy with curly black hair and a shy smile approached them with a steaming platter of grains and chopped roots. The fiery spices brought tears to Sarah's eyes, but the food was delicious. They ate heartily, and gulped down mugs of tea sweetened with honey, until they could eat and drink no more.

As they leaned back against their packs, a shadow fell across them.

'I see you have already breakfasted,' said Rein as he settled down beside them. He playfully patted Will's bulging stomach. 'And you've eaten well, by the looks of this!'

Will giggled and Sarah blushed. Rein's presence had a disconcerting effect on her. His rich voice triggered emotions in her which were at once exciting and confusing. His physical closeness made her feel shy, and to cover her feelings, she rose and searched aimlessly through her pack.

'What are you looking for, Sareka?' asked Will.

The question was innocent, but Sarah felt flustered because she could think of no ready response. Her cheeks burned with embarrassment, and when she glanced up and met Rein's steady gaze, her fingers fumbled and the contents of her pack tumbled out onto the ground.

'Oh, dear!' cried Sarah, and she was horrified to feel tears spring to her eyes. She groped blindly among her scattered belongings, and then Rein was beside her, chatting idly with Will as he gently removed the pack from Sarah's trembling hands and began to carefully fold her clothes. He did not look at her, and Sarah felt her composure returning.

'I wondered,' he was saying to Will, 'whether or not you would enjoy a ride across the plains this morning?'

In spite of her reeling emotions, Sarah laughed as Will clapped his hands in delight.

'We could go right now, before the sun is too high,' Rein continued, 'unless you'd prefer to wait until your breakfast has settled?'

Will looked at Sarah eagerly. 'Do you think we could, Sareka?'

'Well …' Sarah pretended to give the suggestion deep thought. She could see Will was holding his breath. 'Of course we can, Will,' she smiled. 'Let's go!'

The ride was exhilarating. Sarah had never ridden anything more challenging than the ponies at the petting zoo, but Sareka, she decided, must have had some experience because she took to the flying pace like a born rider. She loved the wind whipping through her hair, the quick response of the grazel beneath her, the sheer abandon she felt as she galloped across the wide expanse of the plains with the song of the grasses whirring in her ears.

Will's face was a study in delight. He whooped

and hollered as Meta sprang ahead, clearly establishing the boy as the leader of the race. The cloudless sky was filled with soaring birds. Beside Sarah, Rein kept pace, his face alight with pleasure. He looked much younger and more carefree to Sarah, with his black hair streaming out behind him.

Ahead of them, Will had stopped, and his rippling laughter spilled over them as they raced to draw abreast of Meta.

'Oh, Rein, it's lovely!' Sarah cried as she struggled to catch her breath. She saw her smile reflected in the depth of his dark eyes. She had a sudden memory of Aunt Jenny, sitting on the front porch shelling peas.

'*People who are truly happy*,' her aunt had said, '*smile with their eyes.*'

'What are you thinking about, Sareka?' Rein asked.

'About someone I love,' Sarah replied, and then she coloured at the implication. What if Rein thought she meant ... 'About my Aunt Jenny,' she explained quickly, her face burning once again.

Will trotted Meta closer. 'You seldom speak much about your life beyond the green door. What was it like? Who is Aunt Jenny?'

'She is a very special person,' Sarah said quietly. 'She cares about my world, and she is spending her life trying to solve some of its problems. I never paid much attention to her stories about the rainforest.' Sarah looked out over the broad plains where the last green things grew in Hutanya. 'I will now,' said Sarah softly, and thought, *if I ever see her again.*

'She sounds special,' said Will. 'I would like to meet her some day.'

Sarah was quiet, lost in thought. Rein also said nothing.

'Does it make you feel sad to talk about … about before?' Will asked as he drew his grazel closer to her.

Sarah smiled at him. 'No, not really,' she said. 'It seems like a long time ago. But it doesn't make me sad. I'm not sure why …'

Rein spoke. 'Perhaps it's because before you were there, you were here.'

Sarah pondered his suggestion. 'Yes, that must be it. Maybe this is the first time I've actually thought about it in that way. Before I was Sarah Clare, I was Sareka.'

Rein and Will were silent, waiting for her to continue.

'There has been a part of me that didn't want to believe that, and to accept that this is my home, as much if not more than the world I left beyond the green door. But somehow, now, that has changed.'

Rein had drawn closer as well. He touched her hand gently. 'Knowing has presented you with a great burden. Knowing that you are the one, the only one, who can take up the quest to free the waters.' He lowered his head and murmured, 'I wish it could be otherwise.'

A great winged eagle soared low and pierced the air with its cry. The wind sang in the grasses, and Sarah felt a surge of power rush through her.

'There is hope,' she said, 'and with hope, no burden is too great.' She paused, and breathed in the perfume of the yellow blossoms that surrounded them like a great carpet of sunlight.

'Come on!' she cried, as her grazel leapt to her unspoken command. She was off and racing. She caught the faint cry of Will's voice before it was swallowed by the wind.

'Hey! Wait! Wait for me!'

The ride back was more leisurely. The bees hummed around them and the air was fragrant. Flowers abounded in the meadows of the plains, and their white and yellow blossoms swayed in the breeze. Sarah saw that there were no vibrant reds, blues or violets. Those colours were lost with Hutanya's rainforests.

She felt a restlessness stir within her at the thought, disturbing the peace of the day. The sun was high, and she suddenly yearned for nightfall. She knew what that meant; it was travelling time.

Rein drew his grazel alongside hers and said, 'It will be a fine night for a journey. Only a gibbous moon.'

Sarah smiled. She had forgotten how open her

thoughts were to him. 'Then we leave tonight?' she asked.

'It will be as my Lady wishes,' Rein replied formally. 'The quest is ours, all the people. You are our only hope.' Rein held her eyes with his piercing gaze and this time she did not look away. She saw something wonderful in the dusky pools of brown. It was trust and respect. She saw that he believed she would succeed.

SEVENTEEN

When they arrived back at camp, Sarah and Will found that Archana and Calum were awaiting them. The batlings had been sent ahead to survey the next stage of the journey, and they had not been expected back for several more days. Archana swooped to meet the riders as soon as they were spotted, and Sarah saw that the batling was both tired and distressed. Will called out to Archana, and she alighted on his shoulder, gently brushing her great eyelashes against his cheek in greeting.

'Forgive me, Lady,' the batling addressed her. 'I see you are refreshed and in good spirits. I am sorry to disturb you. We have just come from the north and the news is not good.'

Sarah felt her heartbeat quicken. 'What news?' she asked, with a calm command which she did not feel.

'Sarin has loosed an army of wraiths on the Plains. They are without escort, so the Godawa must have refused to scout for him. That means they are probably already at war. We are all at risk. The wraiths are looking for water, the last reserves of the High Plains. They are headed this way.'

It was decided that they would leave at once and travel by day. Maren and Kay had already eagerly volunteered to serve as their escort to the Teeth, and the grazels were packed to carry them across the first part of the High Plains.

Sarah felt unsettled by the rush to prepare their supplies. She had spoken of her desire to depart at the earliest opportunity, and yet just as she was about to remount the grazel, she felt a curious reluctance to leave.

The Dasai had assembled to bid the journeyers farewell, and she found herself searching among the banners and above the clash of cymbals for someone who was not there.

Where is Rein? she wondered silently.

The Dasai leader was nowhere to be seen, and Sarah was surprised that no one else seemed to notice his absence. As she was turning to ask Maren about him, she saw Lia gesturing to her from the corner of the great pavilion. Sarah excused herself and hurried over.

Lia's beautiful eyes were solemn as she took Sarah's hands quickly and drew her into the shelter of the tent. 'Forgive me, Lady Sareka,' she said, breathlessly. 'I know you depart in haste, but Lord Rein bade me give you this, privately. He begs your understanding. He said he could not come.' And she pressed a small package wrapped in golden cloth into Sarah's hands. The girl continued, 'He asks you not to read it until after you have completed your quest. I am sorry, my Lady, but he made me swear to have your promise of this.'

'I promise,' replied Sarah faintly. 'But Lia, I don't understand. Where is Rein? And why has he asked you to deliver this?' She held up the gilded packet.

Lia bit her lip, and then replied, 'He said he could not stay to watch you leave. He has taken a party south to find out what has happened with the Godawa. I believe he could not say goodbye again.'

'Again?' echoed Sarah.

Lia cast her eyes downward. 'Please, my Lady. I fear I have already said too much. Rein trusts me, and I know and love him well.'

Sarah felt a sharp pang shoot through her at Lia's last words. The message the girl conveyed to her was clear. She understood then that Lia and Rein were already joined by love. She thought fleetingly of the brief and blissful time she had spent with him, and her disappointment welled up within her. She looked at Lia's lovely face and was at a loss for words, but then Lia was embracing her, saying, 'Go, my Lady, and be successful in your quest!' as she gently pushed Sarah back into the crowd.

Sarah was surrounded immediately by the throng of people who escorted her to where her fellow travellers awaited. A cry went up as she climbed onto the grazel and then they were riding across the plains with the windsong in their ears. As they galloped into the sea of grass, Sarah tucked the small gold parcel into the pocket of her pack. She willed herself to quell the hurt that threatened to overwhelm her as she remembered Lia's words … *'Rein trusts me, and I know and love him well.'*

Will, racing along beside her, called to her over the sighing wind. 'Sareka? Are you well?'

I must be, she said firmly to herself. *And so I shall be.*

And she waved encouragingly to Will and gave herself over to the quest before her.

They travelled at speed through the following days to reach the waterholes to the north before the wraiths could swallow them up. They had agreed to send the grazels back after the third day while the animals were still relatively fresh and could cover the distance back to the Dasai camp without thirst overcoming them. The batlings had flown on ahead to scout for marauding troops of wraiths.

It was the day after Meta, Ryu and the other grazels had departed that the travellers crossed a long stretch of the plains where the grasses were short and coarse, singed by the sun's unceasing rays. At midday Kay called a halt to the procession, and they sat wearily on the parched and cracked earth, the wind sighing around them. All of them were weary from the brisk pace they had kept up, and even little Will seemed to wilt in the dry heat.

Maren opened his bag and offered a gourd filled with water to Sarah. She nodded towards Will, and he passed it to the boy first. Sarah watched with misgiving as Will poured the precious water to the ground without drinking. He laughed as it formed a small puddle at his feet. Will smiled up at her, but seeing her frown, his face grew solemn.

'What is it, Sareka?' he asked.

'We cannot afford to waste water, Will,' she said softly.

'But it isn't wasted,' Will protested. 'Look!' And there at his feet, from the hollow of damp earth, rose a green sprout, its leaves unfurling before their eyes. In the centre of the plant, a pale green bud appeared, its petals curling slowly outward to reveal a clump of delicate ruby berries.

Maren's eyes sparkled with approval. 'Will has found the tikki bloom. Once it blossomed every five moons and there was great ceremony in seeking and gathering its fruit. Even in the rainy times it was a rare delight. It quenches thirst as nothing else can. I have only seen it once in my own life and never thought to find it again.'

Will smiled and plucked one of the tiny berries to offer Sarah.

'This is my gift,' he said, placing it in her palm. 'I think you will not be sorry about the water. Eat it, Sareka.'

Sarah smiled. 'You are always telling me to eat something, Will. Sometimes it is a nice surprise and sometimes …' She placed the fruit on her tongue and bit into it. Her mouth was filled with its succulent juices, a sweet nectar which sated her thirst and hunger and brought a flood of images to her mind: the scent of lilacs and pine needles, the hum of dragonfly wings, the sound of a fountain playing and wind chimes tinkling in the breeze.

'Oh!' said Sarah, 'Oh, what is it?'

'Tikki berry, the memory fruit,' explained Maren, popping a berry into his mouth. 'Besides quenching your thirst, it has the power to bring back sense memories.'

Will was nibbling a berry with his eyes closed. A long, loud sigh escaped him, provoking good-natured laughter among the friends.

'Well, Will,' said Kay, 'tell us! What delicious memory have you conjured up?'

Will opened his eyes and grinned. 'Tikki berries!' he cried.

EIGHTEEN

Luck continued to travel with them, and in the golden light of afternoon, the companions reached the last pool of the High Plains. They fell together at its edge and drank the sweet water gratefully.

Sarah lay down on the bank of the pool. The ground beneath her was damp and cool. She dipped her cupped hands into the water and brought them to her face. *Water,* she thought. *How do you describe something that is so essential and yet so common in your life?* She wondered at how much she had changed since she had brushed her teeth and left the tap running that morning so long ago. Water didn't seem common any more. It seemed very, very precious. She dipped her hands again in the pool and scooped it over the back of her neck.

Beside Sarah, there was a loud plop, and she giggled as she saw Ashrok, the lizard, sputtering in the pool before her, his deep croaks clearly indicating his indignation. His yellow eyes glared at her as she tried and failed to stifle her laughter. A spout of water shot into her face, drenching her as she hugged the bank. Still laughing, in surrender, Sarah slid headlong into the pool.

'I'm sorry, Ashrok! I didn't mean to laugh at you,' she called to the lizard as he scuttled indignantly up the bank. 'You see I'm wet, too!' It was the first time she had actually spoken to the lizard. He scrambled off without looking back.

Oh dear, thought Sarah. *I've surely offended him now.* She wondered if she should do something more to appease Ashrok, but the water was delightful, and she couldn't resist gliding across its surface, feeling free of worries and responsibilities, a rare occasion since she had arrived in Hutanya. Her homespun skirt billowed around her as she floated on the surface of the pool.

She heard a cry followed by a splash. She turned and saw Maren standing in the water. He was shaking his long black hair back from his face while Kay stood laughing on the bank above him.

'Sorry, my friend,' Kay called to Maren, 'but I couldn't resist assisting you in!' Then, abruptly, he too was plunged into the water as Will rammed him playfully from behind.

Kay broke the surface in a spray of water, and Will stood, hands on his hips, surveying the bedraggled company. Then the boy sprang feet first in a rainbow of light and cannon-balled into the midst of them, sending water spiralling into the air.

'Well done!' cried Maren, and he reached out suddenly and dunked Kay under the water. The two men wrestled with whoops of laughter.

Sarah drifted to the pool's edge. She caught her

reflection in the water and was amazed at what she saw. A young woman gazed back at her, and in the deep green light, Sarah saw a face with long dark lashes fringing the wide eyes, the high cheekbones glistening with droplets of water. It was a face she knew well. It was Sareka's face. 'My face,' she said aloud.

She grasped the long reeds to pull herself out of the water, and as they parted, Sarah found herself face to face with the long yellowed teeth of a wraith. She froze in terror, and the stench of the creature nearly made her lose consciousness. A scream rose and died in her lungs. Her thoughts reeled. There was something very wrong, even more frightening than the wraith.

Will. Will had not risen from the depths of the pool.

A different kind of terror seized Sarah, a ferocious, passionate Sareka terror that drove all other emotions from her mind. She hissed at the grinning thing before her and its hideous smile died. It scuttled farther up the bank and cowered uncertainly there.

'Wraiths!' she barked over her shoulder to the men, and then she dived.

Below the surface, the silence assaulted her like a wall. The pool was murky and long tendrils of weed whispered like eels at her ankles.

Where is Will? The question thundered in her mind as she forced herself down, her long skirt hampering her movements. Something silver flashed beside her. She felt her lungs ache from the pressure of the water. She knew she must surface soon but fought the impulse, straining her eyes to catch a glimpse of the boy in the now churning pool. She could see no one, and she was forced to rise. As she broke the surface, she gasped in the cool air and wiped the water from her eyes.

She saw Maren and Kay on the far bank; her warning cry had reached them in time for them to clamber out of the pool before the wraiths could act, but they stood helpless within a ring of the ghastly creatures. Will was not there.

Sarah drew a deep breath and was preparing to dive again when the water beside her suddenly exploded in a whirlpool of sound, and her ears were filled with a high, sweet note. Will had surfaced, and at his lips, he held the kalu. Its music rang round the pool, scattering the wraiths like tumbleweeds. They fell back in a tangle of smoke, but held their form.

They are stronger near the Teeth, Sarah thought. *The kalu will not be enough this time.* Still, Will kept the kalu raised high, and the soaring song filled her heart with hope.

Maren and Kay sprang to the water's edge and reached out to pull Sarah and Will onto the bank as the last note of the kalu hung and faded in the air. Will's face was drawn and pale. Sarah wondered what effort it had cost the child to blow the shell so powerfully after rising from the water's depths.

She gently took the kalu from his hand and

raised it once more to her own lips. Pure, clear notes poured from it as she blew, driving the wraiths further into retreat. They scrambled over one another in agony, clutching their skulls and moaning. They would have seemed comical if the situation had not been so serious.

The travellers were trapped unless they could force the wraiths to flee. Only Sarah and Will could tap the power of the kalu, and for how much longer? The effort required to raise its voice drained Sarah and she knew that eventually weariness would overtake them all. The wraiths must have reached the same conclusion, for they gathered together in the distance, and hung on the near horizon like dusty sheets in the growing wind.

Again Sarah blew the kalu, and the wraiths roiled and scuttled backward. Their thin shrieks drifted across the open plains, but they did not disperse.

Maren spoke Sarah's fears aloud. 'This can't continue. They will simply try to outwait us. Wraiths don't sleep.'

'Then I will divert them.' Kay's voice was like a steel blade. 'Maren, Lady Sareka and the boy must go on with you.'

'Oh no!' cried Sarah, and Will grabbed Kay's arm. 'We will stand together,' she said firmly. 'There must be another way.'

Maren's eyes were locked on Kay. Sarah felt a private communication pass between them. Slowly

Maren nodded. 'Kay is right,' he said quietly. 'It is our duty to aid you to complete your quest to free the waters. But it is I who will stay to divert the wraiths, not Kay.'

Sarah felt rather than heard Kay's protest as it leapt into her mind with jolting force. She sensed the great love that bound the two men together.

'No one is to be sacrificed,' she said decisively. 'We must think of a plan.' Three pairs of eyes turned to her, and she knew they expected her to find the solution to their dilemma. She closed her eyes and tried to remember everything she knew about wraiths. Despite their hideous appearance, their powers were limited, even at their strongest. It would be difficult for the creatures to approach their party because of Sareka's presence now that she knew they were there. Their strength lay in stealth and surprise. Sarah had learned from Marwa that the wraiths were like kidnappers, and that they would seize one of the group if they let down their guard, for the creatures were silent and quick. Once in their horrid clutches, it was almost impossible to escape, for their evil was pervasive and a victim soon succumbed to a coma-like condition. The wraiths then took their captive and disappeared, literally vanishing from sight. No one ever returned to tell what happened next.

Sarah drew a deep breath. 'This is what we must do,' she said evenly, although her heart was pounding in her ears. 'We move together — that way.' And she pointed to the ominous creatures that wavered in the near distance.

Kay and Maren looked at her as if she had just proposed they all sprout wings and fly away. They stared speechlessly at her, and Sarah might have laughed if her pulse were steadier and her conviction stronger.

'We're going to fight?' asked Will.

'Yes and no,' replied Sarah. She raised her hand as both Maren and Kay began to protest. 'Listen first, and then if you have any doubts, we'll discuss them.' The authority in her voice silenced them, and she swiftly explained her plan. The course of action was simple. It was risky, but not as dangerous as counting on trying to hold off sleep and the wraiths indefinitely. If Sarah's strategy succeeded, the wraiths would present no future problems. They would be destroyed.

'Are you certain this will work?' asked Kay.

Sarah glanced at Will. 'I am certain of nothing,' she answered quietly. 'It is Sareka's memory that has drawn forth this lore.'

Will reached for Sarah's hand. He smiled up at her, his eyes shining with trust. 'You are Sareka,' he said. 'It will work.'

Maren straightened and turned towards the band of wraiths. He took Will's free hand. Kay offered his arm to Sarah, murmuring, 'If my Lady will permit me?'

Sarah smiled warmly at him as she took his arm.

She felt Will's small moist palm rest lightly in hers, and a surge of light seemed to spread over them all.

'Oh!' said Will.

Despite her fears, Sarah felt calm. 'Oh, indeed!' she said. 'Shall we, gentlemen?'

NINETEEN

The first steps were easy. One foot in front of the other. *Like Dorothy*, thought Sarah, *on the yellow brick road, with the Scarecrow, the Lion and the Tin Man … but who was who?* Her concentration wavered with every step, and she felt strangely light-headed. She made a conscious effort to keep her mind on the task before them. She glanced sideways and saw that the others were also looking confused. Something was not right, but Sarah sensed if she hesitated for an instant, their resolve would be lost.

The plan was simple — approach the wraiths until they were within range and hit them with the only effective weapon they possessed: the kalu. Not its song, but the pearly shell itself.

In her older memory, which had been stirred by Shanila's stories during the nights they crossed the desert, Sareka held a story of the First Turning. A village in Hutanya had once driven away the first force of wraiths by flinging a sacred ornament into their midst. It was not a kalu, but a gourd used in name-day ceremonies, and it too had been engraved with runes.

Sarah's mind repeated a simple chant — *light over darkness, light over darkness* — as she walked resolutely forward. She could not afford to doubt their success. She released Will's hand and felt his fingers curl around her forearm as she slipped her fingers into the deep pocket of her skirt. The kalu lay buried there, cool to her touch. Its smoothness soothed her.

The sun was casting its dying golden light directly into their eyes as they crossed the flat land towards the wraiths. Small puffs of dust rose under their feet, and the travellers were soon surrounded by a swirling brown cloud. The wraiths hung in the near distance, silent and unmoving.

Kay whispered, 'Another twenty metres, my Lady, no more. We cannot risk getting closer.'

Sarah clutched the kalu. Its polished surface was damp from her fingers. She glanced down at Will. His face was still, and she was aware of his intense concentration on the task before them. She struggled to focus her thoughts, willing words of power to her mind, but she still felt fragmented and ill at ease.

Sarah could not make out the deathheads of the creatures in front of them. Their pale eyes and yellow teeth were obscured in shadow, while the sun struck her almost blind in its setting brilliance. Another five metres and she would have to act. She could hear Kay's breathing quicken as the wraiths came within range.

Sarah drew the kalu from her pocket and held it high so that the sun's rays reflected a prism of light from the pearly shell. She called words of power silently to her mind as she prepared to cast their final weapon into the midst of the wraiths.

She was opening her mouth to sing the words, when there was a sudden scuttering at her feet and something green flashed in the dust. Unnerved, Sarah screamed and stumbled, dropping the kalu from her fingers into the dirt. She scrambled to recover it and lost her hold of Kay and Will. Their cries of confusion echoed hers as the brown cloud engulfed them, and then she felt strong arms drag her up and away from the place where the wraiths should have been. As the dust settled, Sarah saw that they had vanished.

Tears of frustration gathered in her eyes. Will squatted close to her, gently brushing the dirt from her hair. Ashrok, the lizard, was beside the boy, with the kalu clenched in his jaws. Sarah watched in despair as he dropped the shell into Will's hand.

'Why, Ashrok?' she cried. 'Why did you stop me?'

The lizard croaked once and then leapt up onto Will's pack and disappeared into its folds.

'I'm sorry, Sareka,' Will said in a small voice. 'He says he wants me to have it. He says I need it.'

Sarah knew there was no use in anger. For whatever reason, the lizard had foiled their plans, and the wraiths had been able to flee. Now they must think of a new way to deal with the creatures.

She saw Kay and Maren speaking quietly together. As the young men approached, their expressions reflected the gravity of their situation. The travellers gathered together in silence.

It was Will who spoke first.

'Now what?'

His question hung in the air like the lingering rays of the dying sun. The wraiths had vanished, but they had not been destroyed by the kalu's power. The creatures lurked somewhere out of sight in the outcrops of rock that broke the horizon, and the travellers were now at greater risk because they did not know where or when the wraiths would reappear.

'I think', said Kay quietly, 'that we shall have to split up. Maren and I will lead them off while you and the boy head for the Teeth.'

'But Will is not supposed to come!' cried Sarah. 'We promised Marwa that he would journey with me only to the foot of the mountains, and then return to Karst.'

They all turned towards Will, who was looking expectantly from Sarah to Maren. He was uncharacteristically quiet.

'I'm afraid …' Kay began, and then cleared his throat. 'I'm afraid I've lost my pack. Will, can you see it? I seem to have dropped it back there in all the commotion.'

Will nodded obediently and trotted off.

'I'm afraid,' Kay repeated, 'that it isn't possible for Will to return with us.' He exchanged glances with Maren, who quickly spoke up.

'Sareka,' said the tall man, 'we must make them think we have Will, for he is what the wraiths are after. When they held us in the ring by the waterhole, they kept muttering, 'The boy. Give us the boy.' We can lead them off, but at some point we must try again to destroy them.'

'And if you don't succeed?' Sarah tasted the metallic burn of fear as she read the answer in their eyes.

'If we don't succeed, Lady,' said Kay quietly, 'we will have won you the time to climb to your quest's end.'

Before Sarah could protest, Will was back among them, dragging Kay's pack behind him.

Kay knelt down beside Will. 'Thank you, my friend,' he said. He slung the worn homespun sack over his shoulder.

'Well then,' Will said once again, 'what now?'

'Now, young man,' said Maren, crouching down beside the boy, 'now, we have a plan and you are the principal player.'

Will beamed. 'I am?'

'Yes, you are,' said Kay. 'You see, we know Marwa gave you strict instructions to return once we had reached the mountains, but we're worried about Sareka.'

Will's face grew solemn, and he looked up at Sarah with concern.

'We all know Lady Sareka has great power, but

she has come to rely on your help.' Maren looked meaningfully at Sarah.

'Yes,' Sarah said, 'yes, that's right.'

'That's right!' Will repeated emphatically.

'And so,' continued Maren, 'we think Marwa would understand.'

'Under the circumstances,' piped up Kay.

'But we want to fool the wraiths into believing that you're coming back with us,' Maren continued. 'You'll need to give us some of your clothes from your pack. We're going to dress this,' he patted the rucksack on Kay's back, 'to look like you.'

'We'll fool them?' Will asked.

'That's right, lad. And you and the Lady will slip right away!'

Will's eyes glowed. He peered up at Sarah in the gathering gloom. 'So I'll help you? We'll climb together and free the waters?'

Sarah bit back the protest which leapt to her lips. How could she decide? How could she know if the choice she made now would be the right decision later? She still had no clear vision of what awaited her at her journey's end. Sarin would be waiting for her. But would he be alone? Could she give him her full concentration if Will were there to defend?

'Lady?' Kay looked up from beside Will.

Sarah drew a deep breath. 'Yes,' she said, 'yes, Will. We'll complete the quest together.'

In the gathering gloom, they fashioned a fair enough imitation of Will. His clothes were assembled around the pack, and Kay held it like a sleeping child in his arms. In truth, Will was now not much bigger than the pack, which aroused Sarah's worries, but there was no time for indecision, no time for delay. They had agreed that they could not disguise Sarah's departure. She and Will wore their long robes, and Sarah wrapped the boy as best she could in the folds of soft cloth which draped over her.

'Please,' Sarah said softly, as she drew herself out of Kay's parting embrace, 'please, be careful.'

Kay joined hands with Maren and smiled, his teeth gleaming against his golden skin. 'We will take care of each other, Lady. You must also guard yourselves well.'

Maren spoke. 'May your quest succeed. May we feast again on the High Plains. May the waters be free.'

The travellers set off on their separate ways.

TWENTY

Marwa lit the torch in the great cavern, and spread his robes on the cave floor. He lowered his body slowly and sat before the paintings of the old forest, his eyes seeking and finding the many creatures which once roamed there and were now no more. The ilix, with curving horns, soulful eyes and its bright flickering tail. The taywa, its yellow eyes peering from a low limb, seemingly languid, but poised to pounce if prey appeared. The quilliks scuttled in the underbrush. Marwa could hear them snuffling and scratching for insects in the tangled roots. He lost himself in memory, breathing the scents of tropical flowers and the pungent earth after a heavy rain cooled the torrid air. He slept.

Rain. He dreamed of rain, great droplets plunking on broad leaves, dripping from their pointed tongues, and increasing in vigour to a crescendo of lashing water. The skies emptied a life-giving flood on the forest. Puddles became pools, and then vast shallow lakes; rivulets grew to roaring rivers, the ground succumbed to the inundation of the rains, and everywhere things were afloat, drifting. Marwa drifted with them, the broken fronds, the snapped limbs, the coarse, fragile soil, all of them travelling towards

a well of rushing sound. The tumult of falling water bat-
tered his senses as spray rose around him in a misted arc.
The Falls! He was coming closer to the mighty Falls, far
away to the north.

The wizard awoke with a start. The fire had
fallen to ash, a few embers blinking beneath the grey
silt.

Thoughts of Will and Sareka drifted through his
mind at random. He saw the girl as a toddler, traipsing
along behind him as he gathered medicinal plants in
the forest depths, her fair brow crowned with a wreath
of red blossoms, chattering in her sweet, clear voice.
She had loved the bird, he thought, and his eyes misted
over at the memory of his lost companion, Myra, the
parrot who had accompanied him everywhere in the
days when Hutanya had thrived, her forest spreading
as far as an eagle could see and beyond.

And then later, after all he held precious had
vanished, after Sareka had disappeared, after the forest
and all her people and wildlife, all her trees and vines,
had shrivelled and died, Will had arrived. The boy had
appeared under the last tree that stood alone in the
wasted land. Marwa had gone there to muster his
remaining power in order to guard the murals, and to
nurse his grief over the loss of all he held dear.

Will had been a mystery to Marwa. The old
wizard had been struck at once by the powerful life
source which emanated from the boy. He knew Will
was a being of the Old Magic, older than Marwa's

memory stretched, and Marwa was very old indeed. The boy was so very alive in a dying world, and Marwa had felt a glimmer of hope, an emotion he had thought was lost to him. So he had taken the child home, and cared for him and taught him all he knew, which was a very great deal.

Marwa had grown to love Will, and he tried not to think too much about why the child had come. Still he knew in his heart that Will was a pawn, a tool that might be used for good or ill. His inner eye soon saw that the boy was the stake for which the forces of evil and good would gamble all. And only one of them could win.

Marwa shook his head as he remembered the sound of Will's laughter, rippling like a cascade of water through the caverns. The old man stirred the fire to life and searched for the sign, but it did not appear. He settled himself back against the cave wall to wait. It would not be long now.

TWENTY-ONE

Sarah did not look back. She had to walk away from the Dasai tribesmen before she changed her mind. A small voice inside her cried, *Don't leave us!*, but she silenced it before it could escape her lips.

Will was wrapped in the folds of her robes, his small head cowled to cover the brilliance of his fair hair. Sarah held his hand as they approached the first rise of boulders that marked the beginning of their climb up the Teeth. The distance between them and the mountains seemed to take ages to cover. Sarah's mind felt numb, and she didn't dare to think how vulnerable they were.

Sarah gazed up at the high cliffs at the feet of the towering mountains beyond. She saw no clouds in the darkness, but there were, without a doubt, wraiths awaiting them somewhere farther ahead on their journey. A chill wind whistled through the crannies of the stone.

As they trudged on, Sarah realised Will was leading her, and had been for some time. She seemed to have no will of her own. The task before her seemed suddenly so overwhelming. *Impossible*, she thought. She stared at the dark stones confronting her, trying to read what malice they had in store for her. She felt nothing but cold, a bitter, unwavering cold, emanating from them.

How, she thought, *am I to defeat a power I don't even know, let alone remember?* No one had told her anything about Sarin, she realised suddenly. Why not? She thought back to her questions to Marwa and Rein, and was struck for the first time by the similarity of their responses. *They changed the subject!* she thought. *Why?*

And then before the impact of that realisation was fully upon her, she wondered, *How am I supposed to free the waters if I don't know what spell holds them?*

They had finally arrived at a very rough trail which snaked up the first of the rocky mountains. Sarah felt so tired. Sleep would be a welcome respite, but she didn't feel the presence of Marwa's gift. Still, she dragged her feet more with each step as they began their ascent.

'Sareka …' Will's voice was a whisper that she felt more than heard. The boy was tugging on her sleeve. 'It's him, you know,' he whispered. 'He's afraid of you. He doesn't want you to come now. He's willing you to turn back.'

Him, thought Sarah. She stood still, as a single thought echoed in her head. *Turn back. The boy can go on. He can complete the quest alone. Turn back. The boy. Alone.* A dark shadow seemed to envelop her. It was not frightening. It offered an absence of feeling.

Sarah sat down on the trail. 'Let's rest,' she heard herself saying. 'Let's wait a bit before we go on.' She tried to gently draw her hand from Will's grasp, but it was held tightly, his fingers clasping hers with surprising strength.

'No, Sareka!' cried Will, and his call echoed back at them as they stood exposed before the mountains. 'It's Sarin! He's trying to stop you. Something you are thinking must be threatening him! I can feel his presence weighing on you!'

As he spoke the sorcerer's name, a lightning bolt severed the sky like a blinding scimitar that fell towards them with raging speed and left the air foul with noxious fumes.

Sarah felt her powers snap to attention, and she instinctively drew Will closer. Cold beads of sweat raced down her back as she fought down terror. The voice in her head was gone.

'Go!' she cried, gathering Will up in her arms. 'We must go on, and quickly!'

She scrabbled up onto a jagged ridge. She realised it was her fear which drove her, an all-consuming fear that propelled her headlong into the last stage of the quest. Not fear of failure, not fear of death, not even fear of Sarin. It was a fear born of love, her love for Will and her desire to protect him at all costs.

She climbed without thought, like a mechanical doll, raising her free arm to pull herself up and placing her feet to follow. Will was silent and grew slightly heavier. He had fallen asleep. Sarah felt no surprise. She held him on her hip, and her mind registered his smallness without speculation.

The fear within her grew sharp and focused. It gave her strength. She devoted all her conscious attention to the rhythm of the climb, and within her, a centre of calm began to grow. There was something else happening to her as well. Something powerful stirring in the depths of her soul. A vision was coming. Sarah felt she had only to wait and the answers she needed would come to her.

She gripped the protruding ledge above her and swung her legs up. She sat still as she rested from the exertion and glanced cautiously around. They were on a path. Something scuttled beside her, and Sarah almost screamed before she caught the flicker of Ashrok's tongue. She had not seen him since he had disappeared into Will's pack after he had prevented Sarah from destroying the wraiths.

'You again,' she muttered. Hearing her own voice, sounding so normal, chased the last of her terror away into the still, cold air.

Sarah breathed deeply and gazed up at the night sky. Knowing was coming to her. She felt the extent of her powers stretch around her like an unfurled sail. She accepted this stage of her awakening with fierce joy.

'*Hai imbrata!*' she sang, and the hills resounded with her song, like a sword stroke ringing against the rock. She expected more lightning, but the echo was replaced by a well of silence. In the quiet, Sarah sensed evil.

Ashrok had scurried ahead, and Sarah saw now that he would serve as her guide up the rugged trail. Indeed it seemed as if he knew the way. Sarah found herself smiling in the darkness as the lizard flicked its glowing tail impatiently.

'Lead on, lizard,' she called softly. 'I will follow.'

The climb was less difficult than Sarah had imagined. Following Ashrok, she could pick out the trail with relative ease, and they made steady progress.

Arden was somewhere above them, but the stars were blocked from Sarah's vision by the rising mass of the Teeth. Still, she had been a night traveller for so long that she could gauge the passage of the time by her own footsteps and the memory of distances she had already crossed. She fell into the rhythm of the climb, as hand and footholds presented themselves to her, almost as though the mountain was encouraging her to make this ascent to what might possibly be her doom. She struggled against this discouraging thought.

'I have no choice,' she whispered, and the sound of her own voice steadied her. 'I have no choice, but neither do you, Sarin.' As she uttered the sorcerer's name, the mountain trembled beneath her feet. She clutched at the sharp rocks to keep from falling. 'Is that rage, Sarin, or fear?' she called. The mountain was still.

Sarah climbed for what seemed like hours, but the night sky remained fixed, the constellations seemingly frozen in position. Then suddenly, Ashrok disappeared. At one moment, he was there before her, and then he was gone. She was alone in the dark. She groped along the face of the mountain until her fingers met a recess in the cliff. The walls within seemed to glow with a kind of green light which rose off the stone. She entered into a small cave.

The strange light revealed a small cavity in the rock face, where she could shelter out of the wind, and it was a good deal warmer. She saw that Ashrok was curled in the corner, seemingly asleep.

'It looks like we're making a stop,' she said quietly, but the lizard did not stir. Sarah silently spread out her bedroll and laid Will gently upon it. The boy was deep in sleep. His rhythmic breathing calmed her fears that he might be under some sort of spell. Only good magic could bring that sort of blessed repose. She studied his resting face and saw no signs of strain. Marwa's gift was well chosen.

As she gazed at the sleeping child, Sarah knew she must come to terms with a truth she had been avoiding since she and Will had first been challenged by the wraiths at the standing stones. They wanted

Will, and that meant Sarin wanted him. Somehow, the child was necessary for Sarin to complete his ring of power. And here she was, leading Will right into the sorcerer's lair! Yet what other choice had been left to her? To send him back with Maren and Kay, with an army of wraiths close at their heels? Sarah knew that she was more powerful, and thus more capable of defending the child.

'I shall have to protect you as best I can,' she whispered. Ashrok croaked loudly, startling her. 'Well, it's more than you seem to have done,' she said to the lizard.

Ashrok rolled his yellow eyes at her, but he remained silent.

Sarah laid a fire, and ate lightly, some chevis and tea. Occasionally Ashrok would flick out his long tongue like a whip, and she could hear him munching noisily on some hapless cave insect. At last she lay down beside Will, drawing his head onto her shoulder. His hair smelled of meadow flowers and the water from the pool. She nestled against him and waited for sleep.

Sarah felt a sort of drowsiness fall upon her, but she did not sleep. The small sounds of the cave, the whisper of Will's breath, a shifting of pebbles from the cave ceiling, were soon drowned out by the rising roar of the wind outside. She imagined it was cold, very cold, but her woven robes kept her cosily warm. The dying embers of the fire cast shadows on the cave walls, reminding her of the great murals in the caverns of Karst. She felt Marwa's presence, and knew he was holding them in his thoughts, and that this was a very powerful magic.

Ashrok had tucked himself under the foot of her bedroll and was presumably asleep, but it was hard for Sarah to tell for sure because his eyes stayed open, protected by a thin, transparent lid. It was only a certain relaxed stillness in the quality of his repose that gave him away.

She heard a faint whirring, and saw Archana and Calum swirl into the cave and dip their wings in greeting. She felt a wave of relief wash over her. *Safety in numbers*, she thought. Not wishing to disturb Will, she put her finger to her lips, gesturing towards the sleeping boy. The batlings settled themselves overhead, and were soon humming comfortingly in their own dreams.

Sarah closed her eyes. The cave smelled damp although it appeared dry. Still, it must have been formed by water long, long ago. She imagined pools of silver on the cave floor, their perfect stillness broken occasionally by a single drop of water seeping through the ceiling above. There were no decorations in this cave; it was just a hollow space in the side of the mountain.

Something may have lived here, she thought sleepily, *back when life abounded in Hutanya. Bears or cave lions of some sort.* She sensed an ancient presence, but it was not threatening. She let her thoughts drift, and hovered between rest and a sort of anticipation. Something was stirring in her mind.

She waited patiently for sleep. Instead, the memories of the past came at last.

TWENTY-TWO

Sareka sat at the council table, to the right of Sarin, as though she were the guest of honour. The shelter was hot, and filled with smoke from the Godawas' ritual pipes. The food and drink Sarin had pressed upon her lay untouched on the platter before her. Sareka was silent, keeping her face impassive, but her anger pressed against her chest like a dammed torrent.

How dare he? Her mind seethed with the unspoken thought. She shifted in the uncomfortable chair, impatient for the council to begin. There was only one topic for discussion, and as far as Sareka was concerned, only one resolution. Sarin had broken the laws of Hutanya. He had upset the balance of nature by using it to gain power for himself, and he had raised an army.

Sareka had travelled to the south to investigate the now confirmed rumours that Sarin had been destroying the rivers and lakes to feed his wraith followers. Marwa had sent her as his emissary to see that justice was done. At first Sareka could not believe that Sarin was capable of such treachery. She knew him better than anyone, and while she was aware he had somehow become involved with dark magic, she could not imagine he had gone so far as to begin using it on such a devastating scale. Months before, when Marwa had first decided to send Sarin south, Sareka had begged the old man to give him one final chance. It was the only time Sareka had ever felt the full extent of Marwa's anger directed at her.

'It is too late, Sareka!' the wizard had thundered. 'He is lost to us!'

'But Marwa —'

'No, Sareka! I will hear no more. He will be sent away, exiled to the hinterlands of southern Godawaland, where he can do no more harm to anyone.' Marwa's face was grim with determination. 'I should have sent him years ago, but I refused to see the truth. Sarin is a bad seed, driven by greed and envy to attain power at any cost.' The old man shook his head. 'How this came to pass I cannot guess. I gave him everything I gave you.'

Sareka had fallen silent. She knew that what Marwa said about Sarin was true. She too had tried to understand Sarin all her life, as she watched him committing small cruelties against those less powerful.

It was during this passage south that she had finally accepted that Sarin was indeed lost to the dark. Once she entered Godawaland, there was evidence of his passing everywhere, the savannahs dry as tinder, the carcasses and bones of animals that had died of thirst and starvation lying in the shrivelled grass. Her horror had given way to anger, and then to a steely determination to stop the young sorcerer once and for all.

And then, on her arrival at the Godawan camp, she had been met by Sarin himself, who had proceeded to act like her host rather than the suspect of a serious crime.

'Ah, Sareka! How lovely to see you again!' said Sarin with a mocking smile. 'Pray, enter the tent and take some food and drink. You must be weary after your long journey.'

Sareka had ignored Sarin's outstretched hand. 'Where is Tor?' she asked.

'Such manners, Sareka …' Sarin murmured, but his grey eyes flashed at her with barely concealed anger. 'The Godawan leader has been … detained. Unfortunately, he won't be joining the council for this discussion.'

'Trial,' corrected Sareka. 'You are here to answer for your crimes.' And she had swept past Sarin into the tent.

As she entered, it was clear that Sarin was very much in control. The mood of the gathered council members seemed light, with laughter and conversation being freely exchanged. There were others in the tent, and the atmosphere was one of a pleasant afternoon's entertainment.

Even the seating of the council was at odds with the usual procedure. Sarin entered behind her and took the place at the head of the table. The three elders, all members of the Godawan tribe, and Sareka, faced one another across it. Sareka had tried and failed to discuss her misgivings about this with Roya, one of the elders, but the old woman and her tribesmen seemed to have been taken in by Sarin's considerable charms and were more interested in enjoying the rich food and drink they had been served.

'Shall we begin,' Sareka said, in a clear, commanding voice. It did not sound like a question, nor did she intend that it should. The murmuring of the assembly, which included members of the Godawa tribe and a few batlings, dwindled to a single voice, as Sarin finished sharing a quiet anecdote with Mir, the elder who sat to his left facing Sareka. Mir laughed, and then sobered quickly as he caught the glint of steel in Sareka's eyes.

Sarin shifted languidly in his chair and turned towards Sareka, his handsome, youthful face politely attentive.

'Of course, dear sister,' he said quietly. 'By all means, let's begin and end this ... *trial* with all speed.' He smiled confidently at the Godawan elders, and was rewarded by three indulgent nods in return.

Sareka's voice was calm but firm. 'Sarin. You are charged with breaking the laws of Hutanya. You have destroyed the waters of Godawaland from its northern borders all the way to Jillian Lake. You are also charged with mustering an army, a force of creatures new to Hutanya called wraiths, for a purpose which you have chosen not to disclose. How do you plead?'

Sarin raised an eyebrow at her and directed his reply to the elders. 'Harsh accusations, wouldn't you say?' he asked in a wounded tone. 'Have you any proof to back them up?'

Sareka saw that he was attempting to shift the focus away from himself. His ploy appeared to be working, as the three elders now regarded her with grave concern.

Mir spoke. 'State your evidence, Lady.'

Sareka gestured to the assembled witnesses, who included two batlings that hung on a rafter overhead. 'The batlings have seen it with their own eyes, as have four members of your tribe. They are prepared to speak for themselves.'

Sareka nodded to the nearest Godawan, a young man with a shy, plump face. 'Come forward, please,' she said kindly.

Sarin's voice cut through her words like a honeyed blade. 'Is this really necessary?' he asked, drawing the elders' attention back to himself. 'I mean, what have they actually seen? Some water has dried up. Unfortunately, these things sometimes happen.' He shrugged his shoulders and smiled benevolently at them.

The elders nodded slowly in unison. Sareka felt the draw of the youth's charisma as well, and brought a word of power to her mind to counteract its effect.

Sarin's head swivelled towards her, and she glimpsed his rage before he veiled it with more soft words.

'Come, sister, do you really feel you need to raise a defence against me?' His eyes belied his conciliatory tone as they burned into Sareka's unflinching gaze.

'I am not your sister,' Sareka replied, 'and you are a liar.'

The elders gasped at this breach of etiquette. 'There is no need for rudeness,' Roya said sharply. 'Lady Sareka, you will confine yourself to the facts!'

'But these are the facts,' retorted Sareka. 'Sarin has captured the waters of the Nina River and all of its tributaries. Jillian Lake is gone. The water has disappeared!'

A batling piped up, 'I have seen it!'

'And I,' said the man who had stepped forward earlier at Sareka's request. He bowed briefly to the council members. 'I am Jas. I have just recently come with what remains of my herds from the south. I lost more than half of my animals. There was no water for them.'

A hushed gasp arose from the onlookers, and Oster, the third elder, leaned towards Roya and murmured, 'I know this shepherd. He is a good and honest man.'

Sareka was watching Sarin. She had not taken her eyes from his since their unveiled exchange. He appeared unconcerned, almost relaxed.

What is he planning? she wondered, and had

barely time to form the thought when the tent was filled with a foul stench.

'Wraiths!' someone screamed, and pandemonium erupted. Sarin rose up, flipping the table sideways, cruelly pinning the elders under its crushing weight. Sareka sprang to her feet just as two wraiths wrapped her in their suffocating embrace. One of them clapped a stinking claw over her mouth to prevent her from singing words of power.

Sarin flashed a triumphant smile at Sareka and said, 'There is still time to reconsider, Lady, if you wish to rejoin the family. Your powers joined with mine would make us invincible.' He cocked his head quizzically as Sareka struggled in impotent fury. 'No? Not interested? I feared not.' He signalled for more wraiths to surround her. The air around Sareka reeked with their fetor.

Sarin took a step towards her. 'I lured you here because I thought I needed you. But I have newly discovered that there is someone else coming who will serve me far, far better. He is not here yet, but he is coming. You are no longer essential to my plans. Unfortunately, I have not yet the means to dispose of you on the spot. I will have to settle for the next best option.' He leaned over and whispered into her ear. 'Unwisely, you have denied me, both as your kin and as your ally. I will do unto you as you would have done unto me. Exile.' The young sorcerer hissed the word at her, and she kicked out at him with the last of her draining strength. He quickly retreated and drawled, 'Actually, I'm doing you a favour. You won't be here to witness what I have in store for your precious Hutanya and its miserable inhabitants. Especially Marwa.'

Sareka saw hatred blaze in Sarin's eyes at the mention of the great man's name. 'You won't remember him, of course, where you're going. It's a shame you won't be here to survey my handiwork. Soon, I will reach my full and deserved powers. For Hutanya, it will be too late.'

Sareka sobbed and bit at the claw that covered her mouth, and almost succeeded in breaking its hold on her. The wraith shrieked in pain, but kept its grip. She felt the small satisfaction of seeing fear replace the smug look on Sarin's face.

'Take her,' he cried, 'and send her beyond!'

Sareka struggled against the loathsome clutches of the reeking creatures, feeling her consciousness slipping away in their malignant grasp. The last thing she heard was Sarin's mirthless laughter, ringing round her like the cackling of demented crows. Then there was nothing.

The second vision came close on the heels of the first. It was very different, more like a bird's-eye view of a tableau being carried on below her. She recognised Marwa, holding a young man who was slumped against him. Marwa seemed to be trying to comfort him, for the younger man was shaking, as though his body was racked with some terrible pain. Marwa's face was still and grey. Then the youth lifted his head, flinging his long raven hair from his eyes. His face was stricken with grief, but even before Sarah saw his eyes, she recognised him by the grace of his movements. It was Rein.

TWENTY-THREE

The vision faded from Sarah's mind, and she lay still in the darkness. Her heart was pounding and she breathed in Will's warm scent to calm herself. She remembered it all, or almost all, as if it were yesterday. Sarin! She knew him as well as she knew herself, but why? The memory of Marwa's words echoed in her head. *I gave him everything I gave you.*

Marwa knew Sarin well, too. Yet he had said so little about him. And before she could begin to ponder the significance of this she saw again the image of Rein, weeping in Marwa's arms. Was he weeping for her?

She felt tempted by the gilded packet which lay unopened in the hidden recesses of her pack, but remembering her promise to Lia, she pushed the thought firmly away. Her joints felt stiff, and her muscles ached. She wondered how much time had passed since she first lay down to rest. Orange flowers of bright embers glowed in the fire, so she knew much of the night still stretched before her. She knew she needed sleep to prepare for the next day's ordeal, and she willed it to come, trying not to dwell on the memories she was hesitant to interpret. Still, despite their disturbing nature, Sarah felt more complete, as more pieces of the puzzle of the past fell in place. She drifted at last into a brief, dreamless sleep.

When she awoke, Sarah felt rested, but she moved sluggishly, and her fingers were clumsy as she prepared an early breakfast of herb tea and sweet grains. Some of the hot liquid sloshed out of her cup onto her hand, and as she examined the small burn, she saw that her pale skin was wrinkled and spotted, and the veins stood out clearly. Hesitantly, she touched her face and felt the lines that creased her brow and grooved her cheeks from her nose around to the corners of her mouth. She drew a handful of her hair over her shoulder, and examined it in the weak morning light that filtered into the cave. It was dull and had lost its shimmer.

'I am old,' she whispered. She was surprised at how calmly she pondered this transformation. She did not feel feeble, nor was she frightened, because she knew these changes had already been foreseen by Will. She gazed down at the sleeping boy, who lay swaddled in her robes. He too had changed in the night. He was an infant now.

Sarah did not wake him. She accepted Will's sleeping state as Marwa's wisdom. She fashioned a sling from her spare skirt in which to carry him, and gently tucked him into it so that he nestled close against her.

Ashrok was waiting at the cave's mouth. He croaked once at her, but appeared unruffled by her changed appearance.

'I am almost ready, Ashrok,' Sarah said. 'Be patient a little longer.' At the sound of her voice, there was a rustling above her and Calum opened his eyes.

'Oh, my!' he squeaked as he caught sight of Sarah.

Archana blinked awake. 'Why, my Lady!' she cried. 'You must be nearly as old as Marwa himself!'

Sarah smiled at the batlings' upside-down stares. 'I'll take that as a compliment,' she replied. She finished stowing her belongings in her pack, and then hesitated. She lifted it gingerly, and laid it carefully in a small recess in the cave wall. When she turned around, she saw the batlings' solemn eyes.

'At my age, I will need all my strength for the last of the climb,' she explained. 'I feel it is not so very far from here to the place where I will meet Sarin. I will return for my pack when I have settled with him.'

The batlings hummed in response, and she saw that they were satisfied with her explanation. Calum made a small fierce sound in his throat, and then squeaked, 'How may we assist you, Lady?'

Sarah was taken by surprise. It was the first time either of the batlings had asked directions from her. She thought for a moment before answering. Finally she said, 'Stay close by. Sarin is powerful, but I believe he is also a coward. He will not meet me without wraiths about. We will need to watch out for them.'

Will stirred against her and she drew comfort from his closeness, as though she were the child she had been when she first came through the green door and Will was her guide once more. She could not afford to think of what the near future held for either of them, for Hutanya. There was no turning back, no place for dread in her heart. It was time.

Ashrok croaked again and flicked his tail, as though impatient to begin the climb. Sarah wrapped her cloak around Will and reached up to gently stroke the batlings.

'Thank you, dear friends. You have served Hutanya well. Be careful.' The batlings hummed softly, and swinging right-side-up, they flew ahead through the entrance of the cave.

Sarah followed Ashrok out into the hazy dawn.

The cold struck Sarah immediately with numbing force, and she quickly drew her hood closed over her face so that only her eyes were exposed to its probing assault. She felt a dull ache begin behind her eyes, and she willed words of power to her mind to combat the dark magic she sensed in the bitter chill.

Incredibly, Ashrok seemed oblivious to the crushing cold. He raced ahead of her at his usual lightning pace, and Sarah sucked in the dry, freezing air hungrily as she strove to keep up with him.

In the pale morning light, Sarah was surprised to find that they were very near the summit of the Teeth. The long night's climb had brought her a great distance before she had stopped in the cave. For as far as she could see, sharp frozen peaks severed the horizon, like mammoth icicles turned upside down under the oppressive grey clouds. Here were the great waters of lost Hutanya, imprisoned in ice for all eternity, unless she could find the key to free them. Marwa had sworn that it was in her power, but she still did not know the way in which the spell could be broken. She hoped with all her being that when the time came, her older self, Sareka, would call forth the magic that would defeat Sarin. Time was running fast.

Sarin had indeed grown in his dark sorcery. With every step forward she sensed his menacing presence grow stronger, and she was shaken by the strength of his power. She concentrated fiercely on gathering her strength, and preparing herself for the task that lay before her, whatever it might be.

Her old bones throbbed with the cold as she trudged up the winding trail. Ashrok's skin had dulled to frosty green in the freezing air. He croaked back at her before vanishing around a bend. As she pushed herself wearily towards the curve, great puffs of steam from her breath encircled her head.

She drew a deep gulp of air into her lungs, and it was then that she smelled them. Five wraiths suddenly loomed up in the path, their deathly pale faces grinning hideously, and a dull, molten gleam emanating from their passionless eyes. Sarah glanced behind her, and saw there were five more of the creatures blocking her retreat. One of the wraiths held something black in each bony hand. Sarah gasped as she realised that it was Archana and Calum struggling weakly in the wraith's vile clutches. Ashrok had disappeared.

She called words of power swiftly to her mind. *'Hai imbrata!'* she sang. *'To tem ingota!'*

The wraiths grimaced, but held their ground. Here in Sarin's realm they were at their strongest. Words continued to tumble out of Sarah, her high, sweet song piercing the thin air. She felt a tremor begin under her feet, and heard the crack of stone splitting from stone. The air was noxious with sulphuric fumes. The wraiths leered at her, but came no closer. She closed her eyes and wrapped her arms tightly around Will, forming a ring of enchantment to protect him in the circle of her song. The sound of rending rock filled her ears, but she sang on.

She sensed the pervading evil recede a little, and she opened her eyes to find herself on a flat pinnacle, one pace wide. The wraiths were separated from her on either side by a treacherous drop. They were gnashing their teeth, and an eerie thread-like wailing rose up among them. Sarah felt the hair on the back of her neck prickle. To her horror, she realised the wraiths were laughing.

'Do you think that will stop us?' one of them

cried, pointing a skeletal finger at the emptiness separating her from the creatures. The wraiths huddled together, and floated in the air above the trail. Those behind her also rose, and they drifted in a pack towards her as she stood exposed at the apex of the narrow peak.

Sarah looked down. The drop loomed ominously. The sky resembled molten pewter, and the cold wind descended with a sharp, biting whine. Sarah thought fleetingly of Marwa. The vision of the wizard's craggy face gave her courage, and she drew herself up and faced the wraiths, who hung in a ragged circle around her.

One of the wraiths turned and spewed a gush of water from its parched mouth. All of the creatures moaned piteously as the flood froze at their feet. Sarah sensed their agony, and realised they existed in a continual state of dehydration. They craved water because they could not keep any for themselves. Sarin's power forced them to find it and return it to him.

One of the creatures scuttled closer to her, and reached out its claw. Fangs of icicles obscured its yellowed teeth. 'Give us the child, Old One. Give him to us, and you are free to go.'

'No!' she cried, and she swiped at the bony hand. Her cloak unfurled, and the cold slithered into her bones. She began to shake uncontrollably. Her vision clouded, and she felt the ring of wraiths move imperceptibly closer. Something, a dark presence, shifted close by. Sarah fought desperately for control of her trembling limbs, hugging the baby to her for warmth for both of them. 'No!' she repeated. 'Never!'

'Never say never,' hissed a sinister voice. It came from beyond the ring of wraiths. They drifted apart to reveal the speaker, draped in a cloak, standing on the ledge. He snapped a whip, and the creatures lay down between him and Sarah, forming a ghostly bridge in the air. He stepped out onto a wraith's back, ignoring its piteous moan, and advanced slowly towards her.

TWENTY-FOUR

His cold beauty sent a shock of recognition rushing through Sarah.

He was tall, with pale silver hair, and eyes the colour of ash. He was dressed all in grey, from his gloved fingertips to his high boots.

'Hello, sister,' Sarin said. 'Have you no greeting for me?' His eyes slithered over her, as she stood frozen as much by shock as from the biting cold. 'You're looking a bit the worse for wear, my dear,' he purred, and he slapped the handle of the whip he held against his gloved palm.

'Sarin. You ...' Sarah struggled to speak what her mind was wrestling to believe. 'You are ...'

The sorcerer raised an eyebrow at her. 'Yes,' he nodded at her, his grey eyes locked on hers. 'Yes, I am. Have you no greeting?' he repeated.

Sarah did not respond. She could think of nothing to say. She was still reeling with the effects of finally meeting, no, *seeing* Sarin again.

'Still lacking in the social graces, I see,' he murmured. 'But never mind. You haven't forgotten to bring your host a gift.'

Sarah followed his gaze to the bundle she held

under her cloak. Fear seized her then, blindly, when she felt his gaze fall on Will, and she hurled words of power at the man before her.

They were snuffed out like faint candles in the rarefied air. The magic had no visible effect on Sarin. Sarah suddenly felt her age, her great age, as a profound weariness seeped into her bones.

'I wouldn't try that again, if I were you,' Sarin said mildly, but his eyes flashed with anger. 'It's a bit late for second thoughts. After all, you've come all this way, and saved me the trouble of seeking you out.' He eyed the circle of Sarah's cloaked arms, and she glimpsed his hunger for Will. He terrified her, but she was also aware that he came no closer. There was a tremendous tension emanating from him.

You must act! she told herself. *It isn't wise to give him too much time to think.* 'I've come to free the waters,' she said aloud in a strong voice.

Sarin's face broke into a leering grin. He laughed, a sharp bark that pierced the air, and then died abruptly.

'Oh, by all means! Be my guest!' The sorcerer waved his hand at the surrounding peaks. 'Only how? It doesn't appear that your singing has any effect. It's certainly not to my taste.' Sarah saw the malice behind his frosty smile. He leaned towards her with the air of a conspirator. 'Shall I tell you what you might have accomplished? Had you succeeded, that is? By freeing the waters, not only would you have saved the miserable Dasai and the mercenary Godawa. The rainforest would have returned as well!'

'But that's not possible, is it?' Sarah whispered, and then caught herself leaning towards Sarin, barely avoiding a headlong plunge off the narrow ridge. 'All of Hutanya died, and what is extinct can never return.'

'Not now, it can't,' Sarin chuckled in agreement. He flicked the thongs of his whip against his thigh. 'Only that old fool, Marwa, knew. When the wraiths came to the rainforest, he had already used his small powers. He had hidden a part of it away somewhere.'

The sorcerer smiled at Sarah's shocked intake of breath. 'Ah, yes, we knew where he was all along, but we couldn't be bothered with him.'

He's lying, Sarah thought. *He hasn't discovered the caves.*

'Of course, now,' Sarin continued, and he nodded meaningfully at Will's draped form, 'now, we will make time.' The sorcerer smiled and Sarah felt her blood run cold. 'Marwa thought he was finished with me when he sent me south,' he continued. 'He found my secret place in the jungle where I kept the crystal and he forced me to leave. But he couldn't change the future. I had already seen it!' Sarin's eyes blazed with anger. 'You were always the favoured one, weren't you, Sareka? I was the elder! By rights Marwa should have given me the attention I was due, but he neglected me in favour of you.' The sorcerer stood clenching his fists, his eyes looking past Sarah as he remembered. 'But I got even. I destroyed Hutanya. Except what part of it that doddering fool preserved. It was the crystal that showed me Hutanya was not totally destroyed. And now,' he smiled at Sarah, and cast a suggestive eye towards the abyss, 'you will be able to tell me exactly where to find it.'

Sarin suddenly snapped his whip. 'Enough of this idle chitchat,' he snarled and reached out. 'Hand over the boy.' He waggled his long, elegantly gloved fingers impatiently.

Sarah felt as though his icy hand had seized her heart. She held Will closer, desperately willing some inspiration to come to her.

'Let's not waste time playing games,' Sarin said, irritation creeping into his voice. 'Besides,' he drawled, 'you're out of turns. All the rest of the moves are mine.' He leaned forward and peered at the bundle beneath her cloak. 'He's an infant, now, isn't he? That's good … so much more malleable.' His eyes raked over Sarah as he added, 'Of course you've had to assume the burden of his waning years tenfold.' He chuckled malevolently, and Sarah felt the air grow even colder.

'You mean, you're responsible for my ageing?' whispered Sarah.

Sarin smiled smugly and said, 'A neat trick, don't you agree? I simply shifted the brat's years on to you. Of course with this sort of magic, there is always a catch. In your case, you received a number of years for every one he lost.'

Sarah tried vainly to still her chattering teeth. 'With what sort of magic?' she asked, aware that she was stalling for time.

'Black, of course,' Sarin snapped dismissively. His eyes narrowed as though he suspected her of trying to distract him. 'Give me the child!' he commanded.

'Why?' cried Sarah, struggling to quell her terror, and to think of some magic of her own which might yet save them. 'What will you do to him?'

Sarin was looking at her speculatively, and his cruel lips curled in a sneer. 'Why?' he echoed, mimicking Sarah's voice. 'Why? Because I need him, and you have brought him to me. I need him to ensure my complete power. He is of the Old Magic, and he is all that remains of the time before memory.' The sorcerer shuddered unconsciously. 'I didn't recognise him until after you arrived. He was the key to the kingdom. He holds the knowledge of the Old Magic within. And I mean to have it from him.'

A sob of fear escaped Sarah's lips, and she silently cursed herself for her lack of control.

Sarin ignored her. He was caught up in his own musing. 'The problem has always been that Marwa got to him first. Filled his starry eyes with all that drivel about preserving the forest, and freeing the waters. That all needed to be undone.' He smiled at Sarah, and she felt her flesh creep at the flame of triumph in his eyes. 'I sent the watcher to make sure he made it here safely, but you did an admirable job yourself.'

'What do you mean, the watcher?' asked Sarah.

'A spy, sister. The lizard.' Sarin smiled with gleeful malice. 'You don't mean to tell me you had no idea? Really, you must have lost all of your powers beyond.' He clucked his tongue in mock sympathy. 'And you don't seem to have improved upon your return. But you have served your purpose. Bringing you back to Hutanya was the most brilliant part of the plan. I needed someone strong enough to bear the child's years.'

'You …' Sarah gasped. 'You brought me back?'

Sarin smiled with pleasure at his own cleverness. 'It was the only way. It was a risk, of course, strengthening the ranks of the Light with your presence, but I needed a sorceress to carry the years I wanted to erase. You were the only choice.' Sarin eyed Sarah with disdain. 'And look at you now. You will never be who you once were, will you? And I will never be who I once was. But then, you don't remember, do you?'

But she did remember. Looking into Sarin's grey eyes, she saw her own face mirrored as it had been in the pool where she and the Dasai had been surrounded by the wraiths. Identical brow, the high cheekbones, the generous mouth. Despite her denial of him at the Godawan council, Sarin was not only her brother. He was more. He was her twin.

Sarin bared his teeth in a wolfish grin, and looked greedily at the child, hidden in the folds of Sarah's cloak. He seemed to be losing interest in her as his desire for Will overtook him.

'You need not fear for his life,' he said, in a sooth-ing tone. 'I want him alive, but I need him innocent, unsullied by any allegiance except to me. He will be my acolyte, my chief admirer. I will turn him to my will.' He raised his fists over his head. 'And then I will rule this land!'

Sarah stared at him in horror. 'You mean to cor-rupt him? To what end? There is precious little life left to rule! You have destroyed it!'

Sarin shook his head at her in mock despair. 'Ah, Sareka,' he chided, 'how little you have learned of the lessons of the world beyond. The land is nothing, life is nothing, without power. There are other resources here besides the paltry stuff you see on the surface of the land. There are riches below the ground, precious minerals that will make me rich beyond imagining, and once I control them, my domain shall have no boundaries. I have made my "connections", as you so quaintly call them. I shall rule Hutanya, and beyond the green door!'

Sarin's voice echoed back from the encircling peaks, and left a hollow ringing in Sarah's ears. She willed herself to block him out, to find the act to free them all from his evil intentions.

'Give him to me!' the sorcerer shouted.

Sarah closed her eyes and focused on her inner sight. If Sarin hadn't taken Will forcibly from her, she thought it must be because he couldn't. She felt the stirring of a memory. A vision of the cavern wall with runes trailing like vines amidst the jungle paintings wavered in her mind. The runes. She could see them clearly and she could read them!

'And it shall be she who comes from beyond the green door who shall strike the desert back and set the waters free. And it shall be he who finds her who will accompany her to the chosen ground, though perilous be every step. And there they will leap before the Great Falls, and all the rivulets, lakes and seas shall follow, and so the land shall be awash in life once more ...'

Sarah's eyes flew open as she felt the hot breath of a wraith in her face.

'That's it, closer,' Sarin was urging it. 'Be careful not to touch the boy, you wretch! He must be pure.'

The wraith reached with a trembling claw for the knot at Sarah's neck that bound the sling in which Will lay. It was clearly afraid of her, but dared not disobey its dark master. Sarin had not moved, and she sensed the fury of his frustration as he pressed the force of his will upon her. 'You have no option, witch,' he growled. 'You must give him to me.' His eyes had narrowed to slits of smoky steel.

'Yes, I must,' replied Sarah, and she watched with satisfaction as surprise, followed by relief, widened Sarin's eyes. She had guessed correctly. Will was only useful to the sorcerer if he was given freely. Did Sarin believe she would sacrifice the boy to save herself? She shifted as much as she could without stumbling over the edge of the precipice.

The wraith's bony clutches still hovered behind her head. It looked uncertainly at Sarin, and the sorcerer waved it back.

'That's better, little sister,' he said. 'Let's be reasonable. After all, I will leave you your life.' He rubbed his gloved hands together in anticipation of having the child in his grasp.

Out of the corner of her eye, Sarah saw that the wraith was still within a skeletal arm's length. Too close for comfort, if her plan was to succeed. She lowered her eyes to centre her powers, and then murmured, 'Allow me to sing a blessing over him.'

'Of course, of course,' Sarin replied impatiently, 'whatever you wish, only make it brief.'

Sarah closed her eyes once more, and willed the words of power to her mind. She called silently on Marwa to join her, wherever he was. She doubted he could see her with his inner eye this deep into Sarin's territory, but the thought of the old wizard gave her the last bit of resolve she needed to carry through her plan.

Sarah raised her head, and looked directly into Sarin's eyes. He was caught off guard as she sang out. *'Hai imbrata! To tem ingota! Hutanya ki alla!'*

This time the words hurled themselves forth. Sarah realised it had been her own fear that had made her words of power fail when she had called on them before. Now the force of her song caused her twin to recoil in horror. It gave her the fraction of time she needed to act.

Sarin's face contorted with fury as he guessed her intentions. He screamed at the wraiths, but they had backed away at his earlier command. He made a grab for her himself, but instead caught the sharp teeth of Ashrok as the lizard leapt between him and Sarah. At that instant, Sarah jumped.

TWENTY-FIVE

The cry awoke Marwa. He stirred the embers of the fire at once. The kindling caught, and flames rose trembling in a spray of light. The wizard peered into the fire's bed, and saw at last the configurations he had been searching for in the glowing ash. The sign! It was the rune, searing its message into the cavern floor. *Hutanya ki alla!*

Sparks ricocheted off the painted walls, and flames spread and lapped at the forest floor in the murals. Acrid smoke began to fill the chamber, and the crackling of the fire became deafening. The cave was afire.

Marwa did not move. He sat on a heap of tapestries, his dim sight now focused on a crimson spot in the vast mural: the red parrot in the great kapok tree, its wings poised for flight. The vivid colours of the mural took new life from the fire's glow. The heat drew moisture from the cave walls, and drops of water sizzled around the old man. Marwa raised his arms, and threw back his great mane of silver hair.

'Hutanya, arise!' he called in the Old Tongue. 'Arise and meet the rushing waters!'

The flickering tongues of the tree snakes slithered in the inferno's light. Wild cats screeched, and ferocious boars squealed at his summons.

'Hutanya, arise!' Marwa's voice was a clarion call. 'Arise and follow!' The wizard seized a torch from the great sconce on the wall. Steam billowed in the cavern as Marwa stumbled in the direction of the cave mouth. Behind him rose a cacophony of bellows, hoots and squawks. The jungle roared to life in the fire's heat, and Marwa could feel the pulse of its life building behind him. Then the last of his spell was released in the fire and the wizard heard the unmistakeable rumble of a tumultuous stampede. Marwa threw himself through the cave entrance and pitched forward onto the ground. He felt the earth tremble with the power he had unleashed as it thundered towards him. He struggled to his feet and, with the last of his strength, flung himself against the cliff face.

The stone was hot under his hands, and an orange glow beamed from the fissures and hollows in the face of the rock.

'*Hutanya ki alla!*' he cried, and then all sound was swallowed in the raging exodus from the cavern. The rainforest was alive.

TWENTY-SIX

As Sarah fell, she heard a deafening splintering, followed by the thundering of something massive pursuing her. She looked above her and where the mountains had been was now a towering wall of water roaring towards her. The Great Falls! She had succeeded in her quest! Their own fate was unknown, but she had freed the waters!

She hugged Will against her, and felt him stir beneath the heavy cloak. She was reaching in to touch him when she felt a sharp sting at the back of her neck. Her hand flew up and met the tentacle of a whip, wrapped around the sling and tugging hard. Sarah could feel the knot loosening, and her struggles to free the lash from its grip caused her to cartwheel through the air. Spray from the plummeting water soaked her as it drew closer. She wiped the droplets from her eyes, and caught a glimpse of a grey shape falling above her, almost engulfed in the foamy tongue that led the waterfall's descent. Sarah felt a sudden thudding wrench, and the sling fell away. She clutched desperately at the cloth. It was empty.

Sarah cried out in horror and struggled to steady her tumbling body so that she could locate Will. Had he been caught by Sarin, or was he falling somewhere near her?

'Will!' she screamed, but she couldn't even hear her own cries over the deafening water, which drew closer. She felt Marwa suddenly in her mind, as if he were trying to tell her something, but his message wasn't getting through.

The thundering water, the dizzying drop and the loss of Will terrified Sarah. She clung to the thought of Marwa like a lifeline. She glanced fearfully above her, but Sarin was no longer in sight. He had disappeared into the boiling foam of the falling water.

When she found the courage to look down, Sarah saw the dusty earth of the scorched High Plains rushing to meet her. It would be only a matter of seconds before she hit the ground. She closed her eyes, bracing herself for the impact, and then felt herself being swept into the icy waters from above, which as they met the land, washed over it in a flooding sea. Sarah was carried along with it, curiously buoyant. Then she remembered the waterproof qualities of her homespun skirt. As she was propelled through the raging water, she searched desperately for some sign of the boy.

'I have to believe he too has survived this fall. I must look for him ahead,' she whispered to herself. The idea of any other fate for Will was unthinkable. She had made the decision to leap, even if it was foretold in the runes. She was responsible for Will's safety. If anything had happened to him …

Marwa's voice intruded on her tortured thoughts. This time, Sarah heard him clearly.

Sareka! Sareka, come home. Your quest is completed. Will is where he should be. Archana and Calum are free of the wraiths.

'Will must be all right,' Sarah cried aloud, her voice shaky with relief. 'Surely Marwa wouldn't call me back if he were still lost or hurt, or …' But she could give no voice to this last dreadful thought, and she turned her attention to keeping herself upright as she was buffeted by the racing sea. It crossed the High Plains, filling in old river beds with spiralling fingers of water, plunging into the lowlands, creating pools and wetlands in its wake. Sarah watched in wonder as the grasses were at first swallowed and then reappeared from beneath the depths. They were growing before her eyes!

She wondered what had become of Sarin. Had he perished or was he, like Sarah, caught up in the flooding sea?

And where is Will?

Even after Marwa's message to her, Sarah kept watch for the boy. Onward she raced with the swelling tide, bobbing like a small umbrella, her sturdy skirt belling around her and keeping her afloat. Her body ached from trembling, with shock and cold. Her legs were numb from the freezing water, and as the hours passed, she gave in to the fatigue which engulfed her. She crossed her arms upon the lap of her billowing skirt and laid her head down. Even the roar of the water could not keep her awake. She fell into a deep dreamless sleep.

When she awoke, Sarah was aware of nothing but blackness, and the steady rushing of the water's current, carrying her onward as it reclaimed its old territory. Then, slowly, a glimmer of starlight caught her gaze, and she was surprised to see that Grona was far to the left, indicating that she was travelling swiftly towards the southern lands. The water's rampage had diminished, and she could make out banks on either side of her. She was no longer at sea, but in the middle of a swirling river. Odd bits of dried weeds and other flotsam occasionally collided with her, or wrapped slimy tentacles around her ankles. The water was warmer now, and the feeling had returned to her legs.

Sarah wondered how Maren and Kay had fared. Had they been successful in eluding the wraiths? Had they been swept away in the raging waters? And what had happened to Rein? Had he done battle with the wraiths on the High Plains?

Despite her fears and weariness, Sarah felt a curious sense of well-being. She had completed her quest successfully, and she could not quell her feeling of pride. Then her thoughts returned to Will, and the accomplishment seemed empty without him there to share it. She felt a sharp pang of loss, and then Marwa's voice was in her head.

Sareka, he commanded, *come home*.

'That's all very well for you to say,' responded Sarah aloud, with a touch of her old irritability, 'but once again, I'm not sure how to get there!'

She realised as she spoke that the sky was lightening in the east. In the gloom that lingered, Sarah scanned the banks for some clue as to where she was, and how she might get herself out of the water. The current was not so strong now, although the river still flowed swiftly. She saw a pile of boulders ahead that rose above the waterline. She paddled awkwardly towards the right bank, and managed to position herself more or less in the great stones' path. She knew it would be a rough collision, but she felt if she did not get out of the river soon, she would be too waterlogged to ever escape.

She braced herself for the impact, and was duly bumped and bruised in her struggle up onto the slippery rocks. She swallowed quite a bit of river water and expelled some angry words, but she gained a precarious grip on one of the bald stones, and collapsed, gasping, across it.

A burst of uproarious laughter startled her into slipping from her tenuous perch, and she had to grapple with the slick rock in order to maintain her hold. She peered furiously through her bedraggled hair into the low undergrowth of bushes, their newly unfurled leaves spring-green in the growing light.

Coughing and choking, she croaked, 'Stop that laughter!' She was rewarded with sudden silence. She lay gasping, like a beached mackerel, her arms and legs dangling over the rocks. She considered how she must appear to her invisible companion, and a reluctant chuckle escaped her. The sheer relief of being on a relatively dry surface after her flight of terror and grief caused the chuckle to well up into a gale of laughter. She found she couldn't stop, and the unknown being behind the bush again joined in, with a deep, booming bass. She heard the bushes rustling, and glimpsed huge hands reaching for her. She was grasped firmly by the arms and tossed over a broad shoulder, and then she was lowered gently onto dry land.

TWENTY-SEVEN

Sarah saw that her rescuer was a giant of a man, towering over her as they both still shook with uncontrolled mirth.

'Thank you,' Sarah managed to gasp as she looked up into the merry face above her. A very big man, with fiery red hair and a full, bushy beard of the same colour, returned her gaze, his brilliant blue eyes twinkling with pleasure.

'You're most welcome, to be sure,' the man replied. He tilted his head to survey his catch. 'I thought that I was the hairiest creature this side of Karst, but you seem to be making a fair bid for that claim.'

Sarah giggled again, and pushed back her dripping silver locks. As she smiled warmly up at the giant, a look of wonder came over his face. The big man dropped on one knee and took her hands tenderly in his great paws.

'Could it be?' he whispered.

Sarah held her breath, willing her own remembrance to come. Feelings first: warm, brotherly, friendship and trust. She knew there was nothing to fear from this man.

'I am Sareka,' she said.

The blue eyes widened in disbelief, and then twinkled again with renewed pleasure. A great shout of laughter erupted from the giant. 'So you are, lass, so you are! But you were disappeared, gone without a trace, the last I heard!' His broad face darkened at the memory. 'I returned to our camp to find it destroyed by Sarin and his pack of spirit rats, and half the tribe spirit-wounded.' He shook his head as if to clear it of the unhappy thoughts. 'Still, you look just the same.'

Sarah shot a look at her hands, which were wrinkled still, but not, she saw, from age. Although the water had shrivelled her fingers like white raisins, her skin was smooth and supple beneath.

'Sarin sent me beyond,' she explained. 'I haven't been back in Hutanya long,' she added, 'and I'm afraid I don't remember everything or everyone from before.'

'It appears you've been back long enough, lass,' said the big man, grinning at the water running past them as they sat on the river's bank. His great head swivelled back to gaze at her again. 'But don't tell me,' he said, 'that you've forgotten your great friend, Tor?'

Sarah struggled to her feet. 'You're Tor?' she cried. 'But you're not at all what I expected!' She remembered her hot words when she had heard of how Tor assisted Sarin in gathering the waters.

Tor must have read the sudden distrust in her eyes. 'So you have forgotten me,' he sighed. 'And you've heard the tales about my alliance with Sarin.'

Sarah nodded, not trusting herself to speak. Tor remained silent as well. Sarah studied his face and saw not guilt or remorse, but smouldering frustration. 'Aye, lass,' he said in a low voice. 'You have indeed forgotten Tor if you believe I could ever have any alliance with the likes of that power-mongering devil!'

Sarah caught her breath in surprise. 'But didn't you provide scouts for the wraiths?' she asked.

Tor's steady gaze met her own. 'Oh, aye. I gave the fiend and his wretched vassals Godawan scouts. And the scouts had their orders directly from me. Lead the cursed wraiths to water, yes, but take them over every hill and dale to find it, and make sure it's brackish and unfit for our own consumption. We led them a fine dance, and bought time for our tribe. I did nothing of which I'm ashamed.'

'I beg your pardon,' replied Sarah quietly. 'I was mistaken in thinking otherwise.'

Tor's hairy face split into a wide grin, revealing sparkling white teeth. 'Well,' he said, 'it looks like that's all in the past now.' He gazed out over the wide river. 'This is your doing, isn't it, Sareka? The freeing of the waters?' He slapped his great thighs with unrestrained glee. 'I'd say this is cause for celebration on a large scale, lass.' He grabbed Sarah's hand and began striding off at an alarming pace. 'This brush is growing faster than I can run,' he called back to her over his shoulder. 'Not that I'm complaining, mind you. Not in the least!' And he let loose another great peal of laughter as he ploughed into the bushes with Sarah staggering in his wake.

The brush was indeed growing before their eyes. Sarah watched in amazement as fronds unfurled and stretched in the steamy air, and she felt the ground beneath her feet become spongy as cushions of moss gathered on its surface. The sun was hot, and Sarah was grateful for the growing patches of shade which were springing up to shield them from its fiery rays.

The big man led her onward, stomping down the creeping undergrowth into a path of sorts for her to follow. She became aware of a tantalising fragrance drifting through the humid air. The smell of cooking fires caused her stomach to rumble loudly, which set Tor off again in gales of laughter. His merriment was infectious, and soon Sarah was begging him weakly, tears streaming from her eyes, to stop a moment so that she could catch her breath.

'I haven't laughed like this in ages,' she gasped. 'I'm sorry, but I simply must stop and rest.'

Tor slapped his knee and gave a great snort, which caused Sarah to double over in a helpless heap, giggling until her sides ached.

'Please stop,' she managed to choke out, and then surprised them both by bursting into tears.

Tor's great hands were gentle on her shoulders as he knelt in front of her. 'Here now,' he said softly, 'what's all this?' He brushed clumsily at a tear sliding down Sarah's cheek, and she saw his own eyes were filled with concern. He patted her shoulder, and mumbled, 'I don't know what I could have been thinking, dragging you along at such a pace. Sure, you must be worn through with your quest and all, and you all alone.'

Sarah sniffled and replied, 'That's just it. I wasn't alone. Will and Archana and Calum were with me. And Ashrok,' she suddenly remembered. Sarin had said Ashrok was the watcher. But it had been Ashrok who had saved Sarah from Sarin's grasp. Sarah tried to remember if she had seen the lizard fall. 'What's happened to Ashrok? Marwa sent me word of the others, but he said nothing of Ashrok.'

'Hush, now,' said Tor soothingly. He lifted her in his strong arms and she realised she was exhausted. She rested her head gratefully against his broad chest.

They entered the camp of the Godawa in what seemed to be just a few strides of Tor's long legs. The big man shook his fiery head furiously when a crowd of people gathered around them, all calling questions at once. Silence descended respectfully as the tribe peered at Sarah's seemingly lifeless form. Despite her weariness, Sarah could not suppress a chuckle as she opened her eyes to see the solemn faces hovering over her. At the sight of her smile, the questions began again, at first in whispers, and when Tor said, 'Sareka!' a great roar exploded from the assembled group that surely, Sarah thought, would have raised even the dead.

Later, after a delicious meal of smoky beans and flat bread, Sarah told the tale of her quest to the Godawa. The tribe listened attentively, and made comments of approval, admiration, or dismay as she related each stage of her journey.

After she told them about her leap from the Teeth, Tor said, 'The wee boy must have gotten by us. I shouldn't fear for him, though, lass, being as he is of the Old Magic. The same with those batlings. Old Marwa knows what he's about, and if he's told you they are safe, then safe they must be.'

Sarah smiled gratefully at Tor. She felt a strong bond of kinship with him, and his level-headedness comforted her greatly. The increasingly heavy air and the growing warmth made her drowsy, and she dropped onto her sleeping robes with a strong desire to sleep for at least two hundred years. As her eyes fluttered closed, a disturbing thought intruded. She thought back on what Marwa's message had been. What was it he had actually said?

Sareka, come home. Your quest is completed. Will is where he should be. Archana and Calum are free of the wraiths.

The wizard hadn't actually said her companions of the quest were safe.

TWENTY-EIGHT

The plan was to set off for Karst at first light. The day began with twittering and buzzing, which swelled to a symphony of hoots, chattering and snuffling. The growing trees rustled with life. Sarah saw in the morning light that the camp was located at a bend in the river, and here the water ran gently enough for her to enjoy an early morning dip.

She dived into the cool depths of the coffee-coloured water, rose to the surface and floated on her back, enjoying the vibrant shades of green which were still unfurling before her eyes on the branches overhanging the river banks. The river soothed her aching body, which had been jostled and jarred during her journey. Even not having Will to share her triumph seemed less important now. She would see him again soon, she felt sure.

She was startled from her thoughts by a tremendous splash which sent a wave washing over her. Tor's shaggy head broke the surface, and he spouted a fountain of water from his mouth.

'Ah!' he exclaimed. 'The water is truly delicious! Thanks to you, lass.' Rivulets of water poured down from his bushy eyebrows onto his ruddy cheeks. 'I imagine you'll be keen to head for home.'

Home, thought Sarah. *Where is that now?* She thought of the memories she had gathered since she arrived in Hutanya, of her lost childhood with Marwa in the forest which would now be returning to Karst. She thought of her mother and father beyond the green door, and Aunt Jenny and her baby soon to be born. And she thought of Will. No clear answer came to her.

'I'm ready to head for Karst when you are,' Sarah said. 'How long a journey will it be?'

Tor rolled onto his back like a great whale. 'Now that the rivers are running, it will be only one day. If we leave as soon as we've eaten,' and he patted his big belly appreciatively, 'we should be there just after nightfall.'

A scream broke the air, causing Sarah to clutch at Tor's arm. He gave a shout of laughter. 'Have no fear, lassie. It's a taywa calling to her mate. They're all coming back, all the animals. It's a miracle ... a miracle that I imagine old Marwa had something to do with.'

Sarah remembered the murals on the cavern walls, and the tawny cats that lay in the trees, their great paws and tails dangling languidly from the branches. Marwa had succeeded in his quest, too. He had preserved the life of Hutanya until the environment could support it again. She felt a sudden longing to feel his old strong arms around her.

'Let's eat,' she said, as she climbed up the slippery bank, 'and be on our way.'

'As you wish, lass,' replied Tor, lumbering after her. 'I'm so hungry I could eat a grazel!' And seeing Sarah's look, he added quickly, 'Just a figure of speech, lassie, just a figure of speech!'

They set off, just the two of them, in a sturdy craft which had been carefully maintained over the long seasons of drought. Someone, thought Sarah, had believed that Sarin could be defeated. She suspected that someone was Tor.

The river flowed from south to north east, which suited them perfectly, for it would lead them right to the heart of Karst, and quite near, by Tor's reckoning, to the caverns where Marwa had sheltered Sarah less than a moon ago. Sarah realised she must have drifted past the caves in the rushing torrent the night before. So much had happened in such a short time!

Their surroundings continued to change dramatically before their very eyes. The river ran swiftly, but not so fast that Sarah couldn't marvel at the beauty around them, at the blossoming of the giant rakkias, huge purple flowers which unfolded on the trunks of trees stretching closer to the sky. A canopy of soft fluttering green was closing over their heads, and the water was dappled with light and shadows. Sarah breathed in the air heavy with the scent of damp earth and fragrant flowers. They travelled to the music of birdsong and the chattering of small primates and parrots in the trees.

Sarah felt a growing excitement. She would soon be back in Karst, and be reunited with Will and Marwa. She wondered if Marwa still kept to the caves, but couldn't imagine anyone being able to resist the lure of living amid the teeming life the new Hutanya offered. And what must Will think of all these colours? She smiled to herself as she imagined his small figure bounding about in pleasure. She stopped mid-thought, remembering that he had been an infant the last time she had seen him.

She leaned over the side of the boat and tried to catch a glimpse of her reflection in the water, but they were moving too quickly. She knew she was no longer old, and decided by her height and body shape that she had returned to the age she had been when she was with Rein and the Dasai. She wondered if Will was gaining years as she was losing them.

At the thought of Rein came a now familiar ache in the region of her heart. She missed him, and wondered what had become of him in the battle with the wraith army. Tor had told her that the wraiths had been defeated — they had actually drowned themselves in the waters — but that many a brave Dasai and Godawan had been gravely injured in the terrible fight before the rivers reached the land.

'We joined forces with the Dasai at the border between Karst and the High Plains. Ach, it was a terrible fight,' he had told her in a hushed voice the night before, and his blue eyes had filled with tears as he recounted the horrors of battle. 'The wraiths cannot kill, but their touch is like a poison which eats into the spirit. Only those with some protection of the Old Magic can repel its evil force.'

Sarah had remembered the visions she had seen in the cave on the Teeth, and the paralysing power of the wraiths as they had gripped her at the council table before Sarin had sent her beyond. She wanted to ask Tor about Rein, but she dared not, for she was afraid to know if something had happened to him. She was afraid of what she already felt for the man whom she could only consider a friend, since she had learned of his close relationship with Lia.

'Look ahead there, lass,' Tor called from the stern of the boat, interrupting her thoughts. 'Beyond that big bend in the river is the beginning of Karst.'

Sarah watched as the boat rounded the bend, and saw with delight, above the treetops, the familiar orange cliffs of Karst looming in the distance.

'Oh, Tor!' she cried out. 'It is Karst! I didn't think I'd recognise it, with all the new growth. I can't wait to see Marwa and Will!' She caught sight of Tor's wide grin and added sincerely, 'Of course, I've been so happy to see you again.'

Tor chuckled and said, 'Aye, lass. I know you have. But there's no place like home.'

Sarah grew quiet and thought about his words.

Home. Was this it? When would she know? Marwa had told her she would be able to go back beyond the green door once her quest was completed. But did she want to? Was she still Sarah Clare or was she Sareka?

As the afternoon slipped into twilight under a bower of early stars, Sarah pondered the questions in her mind. The cliffs of Karst were near, and soon they would begin to search for a landing on the bank. Perhaps once she was in Karst she would be sure.

TWENTY-NINE

The light died quickly, swallowed up in a momentary stillness which was suddenly filled with a rush of insect voices. They secured the boat to an overhanging branch on the river bank, and Sarah stepped into the forest. She heard the familiar squeaks of batlings, and she called out impulsively, 'Archana! Calum!'

There was a great fluttering of wings, and Tor and Sarah were surrounded by a black sea of batlings. A bright-eyed female that Sarah recognised as Hetreena brushed her cheeks in greeting, and the hum of the batlings' pleasure vibrated in the air.

'Welcome home, Sareka!' Hetreena squeaked. 'We have been watching for you since the waters were freed.' The batling dipped her wings to Tor. 'Welcome to you, Tor of Godawa! It is long since we have had the honour of your presence in Karst.' She fluttered shyly and brushed the great man's hairy cheek in greeting. 'Come, please. You are awaited by Marwa.'

'And Will?' asked Sarah, as she hurried beneath the sea of batlings. 'He is here, isn't he? With Archana and Calum?'

There was the tiniest of pauses before she heard that old infuriating response of her batling friends from before the quest. 'That', squeaked Hetreena, 'can best be answered by Marwa.' And she flitted on ahead.

A small knot of fear clenched in Sarah's stomach. She stumbled in her haste over roots underfoot, and was prevented from falling headlong by Tor's firm grip on her elbow. His burly presence calmed her, but the knot of fear grew to a fist as she stepped into a clearing lit by torchlight and the brilliant night sky.

Marwa stood alone before her, a bright red parrot on his massive shoulder. His ancient face was creased in deep furrows. He hurried forward and wrapped her in his embrace. Sarah clung to him as he stroked her hair and murmured, 'Well done, my child. You have saved Hutanya. We are honoured to receive you.'

Sarah felt Marwa's lips brush her brow before he held her away to look at her. 'You have grown quickly,' he said.

Sarah's heart pounded loudly in her ears. She was afraid to move, to speak, to ask the question.

'Archana and Calum are on the High Plains,' the wizard said. 'They are still recovering from their encounter with the wraiths, but I believe they will soon be well. The Dasai are great healers, and now that the forest is returning, there will be an abundance of medicine. I too have benefited from Sarin's defeat. I have recovered my sight.'

Sarah read the answer to the question she had not yet asked in the old man's blazing blue eyes. The gripping fear which had receded as she fell into

Marwa's arms now swelled within her, threatening to swallow her whole.

'He's not here?' she whispered.

Marwa's great hands rested on her shoulders gently. His eyes held hers like a candle flame holds a moth.

'Listen to me, Sareka,' said Marwa softly. 'He was never meant to return. I knew it, but I didn't want to believe. I knew it the first time I saw you in the great cavern. I remembered what was written in the runes.' The old man smiled through the tears that were gathering in his eyes. He shook his head slowly. 'I should have told you. I am sorry.' Then he raised his great head and quoted in a strong voice.

'And it shall be she who comes from beyond the green door who shall strike the desert back and set the waters free. And it shall be he who finds her who will accompany her to the chosen ground, though perilous be every step. And there they will leap before the Great Falls, and all the rivulets, lakes and seas shall follow, and so the land shall be awash in life once more ...'

The words rang through the air, and the forest fell silent. Sarah stood before the wizard, her eyes locked on his, struggling to understand what her mind refused to believe.

The wizard continued. 'But there was more ... *so the land shall be awash in life once more. And one shall return and one go on before.'*

And one go on before. The words echoed in

Sarah's head, but she could find no response.

'I didn't know for sure which of you it would be who would return,' continued Marwa, 'until I felt your mind casting about for Will after you leapt from the falls. Then I knew he was the one who went on before.'

'You mean …?' Sarah sobbed, unable to say the words aloud.

Marwa sank to rest against the base of an old tree. It was the scraggly one that Sarah had first seen when she had come through the green door, now clothed in shiny new leaves. He reached out his hand and drew Sarah down beside him.

'I remember when he first came to me,' he said softly, as he stroked her glimmering hair. 'He just arrived one day, under this very same tree where the door appeared to bring you back to us. He couldn't say where he was from, he just *was* when I found him. Just Will.'

The old man shook his head. 'It's odd,' he continued. 'I was grieving then, as I am now. I was missing you, Sareka.' He lifted his great, shaggy brows and looked directly at Sarah. 'All life has its cycle, my dear. I thought you were lost forever, but here you are.' His face broke into a thousand wrinkles as he smiled at her. He opened his arms, and she fell into them. Another great sob escaped her throat, and she was engulfed in her sorrow. Marwa held her, rocking her gently in his strong embrace. 'Let it go,' she heard him murmur. 'Let your sadness flow out of you, as the river to the sea.'

Sarah wept until her tears were spent. After a

time, she fell silent, still in the comforting circle of Marwa's arms. She felt cleansed by the release of her emotions, as if she had laid down a heavy burden. She knew she would grieve for Will, and carry him in her thoughts always, but she felt something within herself willing her not to give in to sorrow and remorse. It was a powerful force which welled up inside her, and it was echoed in the forest's return to burgeoning life.

'What about Ashrok?' Sarah asked quietly. 'Sarin said he was a spy, a watcher.'

The sorcerer sighed. 'Ah, Sareka. I have much to beg your forgiveness for. Sarin first.'

'My twin brother,' said Sarah.

'I know I should have prepared you. I was afraid the thought of destroying your twin, before you had awakened and had remembered, would keep you from accepting the quest. I am sorry to have withheld this information from you.'

'You did it for the good of Hutanya,' said Sarah. 'There is nothing to forgive.'

Marwa patted her hand gratefully. 'Ashrok was the watcher, was he?' And Sarah was surprised to hear Marwa chuckle. 'Sometimes that boy was such a fool!'

'Who?' said Sarah. 'Will?'

'No!' said Marwa. 'Never Will. No, I meant Sarin.'

'Why?'

'Because if he had ever paid any attention to the powers of the forces of Light, he would have known that a creature such as Will, of the Old Magic, can never be corrupted. And any creature who is corrupt, perhaps as Ashrok once was, would be released from dark magic once it formed a bond with Will.'

'But that means Will couldn't have helped Sarin gain the power he needed!' cried Sarah.

'Most assuredly not,' agreed Marwa, his face once again drawn and grim. 'The boy believed everything he saw in that crystal. But the crystal only reveals one version of the future. Nothing is ever determined alone. Good and evil exist, and each can sway the path ahead. But in the end each soul must decide which side to follow. And that can make all the difference.' The old man smiled down at Sarah. 'As indeed it has.'

'Is Ashrok with Will?' Sarah asked in a small voice.

'I am certain he is. Those two companions will always be together,' said the wizard.

Sarah rested her head in the crook of Marwa's arm. 'Do you know where Will is?' she whispered.

Marwa paused so long before answering that Sarah thought he hadn't heard her. Finally he responded in a low voice. 'No. I don't. He must have returned to wherever he was before he came to Karst. He is of the Old Magic. I cannot feel him anywhere in Hutanya. Except in my heart.' The sorcerer tapped at his chest as he smiled at Sarah. 'Except in my heart.'

THIRTY

Sarah and Marwa talked long into the sultry night under the bright sky.

'What have you decided?' asked the wizard finally. 'About returning beyond?'

Sarah leaned back against the rough bark of the tree. She thought about all her friends and her renewed memories of past happiness in Hutanya. She imagined spending her days in the beauty of the forest, and wondered what she still had to learn about herself as Sareka. She thought of Rein, and of Will, and felt that she would learn to deal with her sense of loss in time.

And then she thought of Sarin.

'*I have made my connections*,' he had said. In Sarah's world. Even if Sarin had died in the fall, there were still forces like his at work in the world beyond the green door, forces which could lead to a similar destruction.

'I have to go back,' Sarah said decisively. 'I think I may be needed.'

Marwa patted her arm. 'I thought so,' he said.

'Do you think Sarin survived the fall?' Sarah asked him.

The wizard sighed and shook his head.

'Unfortunately I have no idea. I suppose we shall know soon enough, although his power is greatly diminished with the last of the wraiths gone.' The wizard looked deeply into Sarah's eyes. 'Anyway, I expect you'll be back here in Hutanya before too long if we should need your help again. See that it's not too long, Sareka, won't you?' he said with a touch of his old gruffness. 'These old bones won't last forever, you know.' Sarah's dismay must have been apparent, for the old man growled, 'Now don't get the idea that anything is going to happen to me for at least the next five thousand moons or so!'

Sarah begged Marwa to let her spend her last night in Hutanya in the caves. The beauty of the forest, resplendent in bold colours, made her miss Will more. How the boy would have loved it! The mysterious screeching and hooting, and the scratchings and scut-tlings in the undergrowth would have provided him with endless explorations. The heady scents of jasmine and frangipani would have delighted his sensitive nose, and she could imagine him gorging himself on the suc-culent fruits of the trees. It would have been a playland beyond his wildest dreams. But she sought the solace of the caverns, their walls now vacant and grey in the torchlight. The stillness kept her thoughts of Will from overwhelming her with sadness.

Marwa led her to the place where she and Will had laid their sleeping robes less than a moon ago. Cushions were scattered on the cave floor, and a cooking fire was already crackling, for although the forest outside was tropically warm, the caves had retained their cool climate.

They had a simple meal, and sat in silence afterward, sipping tea sweetened with honey from the High Plains. Sarah's thoughts flew to Rein, and the brief, happy time she had spent there with him.

As if reading her mind, Marwa spoke. 'Rein was successful in preventing the main army of wraiths from reaching the southern lands. He met them on the northern borders of Karst, and dispersed them.'

'How did he defeat an army of wraiths?' asked Sarah.

Marwa chuckled. 'With a pure heart. Rein sang in the Old Tongue and called the forces of goodness to aid him. And little Lia proved her bravery as well. She stood by his side against the horrid creatures. Of course, once the waters were freed, it was all over. The sight of all that liquid broke Sarin's hold over the wraiths. They drank themselves to death.'

Sarah's heart felt squeezed a size smaller at the mention of Rein and Lia together, and she was ashamed of herself for the jealousy she could not deny. Lia had been a friend to her, and she knew she should wish the couple well. She looked up from her tea to see Marwa's azure eyes looking at her quizzically, and she hastily covered her thoughts by asking the wizard about his parrot, who seemed to have attached itself permanently to his shoulder.

Marwa turned and addressed the bird fondly. 'Good heavens,' he said, 'don't tell me she doesn't remember you, old girl!' He tapped the parrot affectionately on its beak, and turned to Sarah. 'You've known Myra since you were a wee bit of a thing, even younger than Will was when he arrived at the caves.'

At the mention of the boy's name, they grew silent again. Sarah stared into the fire, holding the vision of Will's sweet smile like a talisman against her despair. She heard the rustling of Marwa's robes, and then she felt his great roughened hand pat hers as he rose to go.

'Settle in among the cushions, and try to sleep,' the wizard murmured. 'I will come for you at dawn.'

Sarah dozed lightly, but something woke her. She sat up and poked at the fire, and watched the shadows dance in the empty cavern. She noticed a lump at the foot of her sleeping robes which had not been there before. She reached for it, and gasped in wonder. It was her old backpack, which had travelled with her from these caves to the Teeth.

But she had left it stowed in the small cave in the mountains where she had sheltered on her last night with Will.

'How did this get here?' she said aloud, and she was startled to hear a delightfully familiar voice answer her from the shadows.

'I brought it.'

Sarah scrambled to her feet as Rein stepped

into the torchlight. His raven hair shone around his shoulders, and his eyes were a rich mahogany, the colour of the river that ran past the cave entrance. He held her in his intense gaze, and she could not move.

'I found the pack on the banks of Jillian Lake,' he said.

Sarah found her voice. 'The floods must have washed it down from the Teeth.' Her heart was making sudden lunges against her chest, which she was sure that Rein could hear, or maybe even see.

Rein took a step towards her. She still could not move, and stood like a deer frozen in a sudden light. It wasn't until he reached out to touch her cheek that she stirred, ducking his hand and moving a step away. As she turned to tend the fire, she could not help but see the confused hurt that flashed in Rein's eyes.

'Forgive my lack of manners,' she said, hastily plumping a pillow. 'Please. Sit down. You must be tired.' Her eyes travelled over his stained clothes. 'Have you come just now from the High Plains?'

'No,' replied Rein. 'I was on my way to Godawaland. I met Tor on the river and he told me you were here.'

'Tor has already gone back to Godawaland?' cried Sarah. 'I didn't get a chance to thank him, or say goodbye.'

Rein sat down slowly beside Sarah, and she felt the power of his gaze draw her eyes like a magnet, but she fought the impulse to look at him. 'Marwa says you plan to leave in the morning,' he said.

Sarah nodded, still not meeting his eyes.

'Sareka,' he said softly. 'I …' His voice broke off as she turned away to prepare tea. She was aware of his closeness, and then she felt his strong hands grip her shoulders, and he turned her to face him, his dark eyes blazing. She saw a look she could not read, dared not believe.

'How is Lia?' she blurted out, and she felt his hold on her slacken.

'She is fine, but she is not who I came to speak with you about. Sareka, I …'

'I'm glad to hear it,' Sarah said, 'and may I wish you every happiness.' She felt tears stinging her eyes, and blinked furiously.

Rein released her, and stared quizzically at her. 'I will convey your good wishes to my sister. Now will you let me speak?'

Sarah felt as though she had been struck by a bright ray of sunlight, although the cave remained shadowed in the flickering torchlight. She knew she was standing with her mouth open, and that she probably looked ridiculous, but it didn't seem to matter very much. And suddenly she was seized with a fit of giggling. Lia was Rein's *sister!*

'Sareka? What is it?' Rein was looking at her with frank confusion on his face. He smiled, and then frowned uncertainly. He reached down and picked up her worn pack, and thrust it at her.

'Here,' he said simply. 'You haven't opened my gift to you yet.'

Sarah choked back her laughter and accepted the pack. 'Your gift?' she said. 'I thought it was a letter.' She rummaged in the bag, all the while feeling the light fill her heart. She was aware that Rein scuffed his feet uneasily beside her, and smiled to herself. *This time he is the one feeling awkward and shy*, she thought.

The golden parcel was in the inner pocket of the pack, its glittering wrapping only slightly creased by the rough journey. Sarah held it in the palm of her hand and looked at Rein directly. His eyes were hooded by the dark sweep of his lashes, and she could not guess his thoughts completely, but she felt his tension in her mind as clearly as if he had spoken of it aloud.

'What is it?' she asked him, but he simply shook his head and gestured to her to proceed.

'Open it,' he said, 'and see.'

Sarah gently loosened the gilt ribbon that held the parcel closed, and peered into the folds of cloth in which the gift lay. It was a tiny kalu on a slender gold chain.

'Oh, it's beautiful!' Sarah cried, and she lifted it from the wrapping and examined the rune. She recognised it at once, and her eyes locked on Rein's as she realised the gift's significance. Slowly she fastened the chain around her neck. At the instant she closed the clasp, she heard Rein release his breath.

His face was still, his strong features softened in

the shadows. She felt his presence from within and without. She walked towards him, until she stood directly in front of him.

'Be my mirror now, Rein,' she said. She stared into the tall man's dark eyes, and saw the pearly glint of the kalu, like a moonbeam, reflected in their depths.

'I must return to the world beyond the green door,' she said softly. She could feel Rein's emotions reeling round her like cartwheels. 'But I know what your gift means, and I accept it. I will be back.'

Sarah felt Rein's breath, warm and sweet against her hair as he gathered her into his arms. She reached up and cupped her hand around his cheek, and drew his face down close to hers. They kissed gently, a kiss of greeting and a kiss of farewell. Both of them were aware of holding back the passion of their feelings for one another. That kiss was for a future time together.

'You understand the gift?' asked Rein, as though he was afraid there had been some mistake.

'I know the rune. It says *promise of love.*' Sarah blushed as she said the words aloud. 'And I know that it means we will be together, for all time, even if we are apart for a while.'

Rein stroked her long shimmering hair. 'I will wait for you,' he said, and Sarah heard the fierceness of his love in his quiet voice. 'I can only pray it will not be so long this time.'

Sarah remembered her vision of Rein grieving in Marwa's arms. 'Were we promised before?' she asked.

'No,' replied Rein. 'We agreed to wait until you returned from the Godawa Council. Do you have no memories of us?'

Sarah let her mind open and drift. She saw no visions, but laughter echoed in her thoughts, and the feeling of light that seemed to stream into every pore was growing stronger. 'I remember I was happy with you,' she replied.

'We will be happy again,' Rein said. There was a silence before he spoke again. 'I know not all of this time in Hutanya has brought you joy. I miss Will, too. I think of how much he would have loved Hutanya as it is becoming again.' He rested his cheek on the top of Sarah's head. 'But I think he would be sad if we cannot enjoy it because he is not here. He would want us to celebrate the rebirth of the land.'

'I feel that, too,' said Sarah quietly.

They sat down together and watched the flickering of the fire as it played against the cavern walls. Sarah felt a familiar drowsiness as Marwa's gift came to her for the last time.

THIRTY-ONE

Sarah awoke to find herself on the cushions, wrapped in a finely woven blanket. Rein was asleep, sitting up against a wall of the cave as though he had guarded her through the night.

Marwa appeared at the mouth of the passage and called softly, 'It is time.'

Rein's eyelids fluttered open, and he rose to help Sarah tidy the cushions before they followed Marwa to the outside. They did not speak, but their fingers brushed together, and Rein clasped her hand fast in his.

There was a drumming sound which grew louder as they walked down the dark tunnel to the opening in the cliff walls. It was strange and familiar at the same time to Sarah's ears. As she stepped out into the open, she realised it was raining. Great drops of water were thundering down from the cloudy sky, and she was instantly soaked.

In the next moment, she was being hugged enthusiastically by two people at once, both of them as drenched as she was.

'Kay! Maren! Oh, how wonderful! You're all right!' Sarah threw her arms around them both. Then she drew away saying, 'Here, let me get a proper look at you. *Are* you all right?'

The two men started to speak at once, and then they were all laughing together. Kay reached out tentatively and lifted the chain around Sarah's neck. When he saw the kalu, he let out a delighted whoop, and then he began thumping Rein's back while Maren picked up the young man and swung him around.

A great roar rose above the pounding rain, and Sarah became aware that there were others, many others, surrounding them in the clearing.

'Oh, my!' she said, as she turned slowly in a circle, taking in all of the assembled people and creatures. She saw Shanila and Lia, and many more familiar faces from both the Dasai and Godawan tribes. She saw the batlings and cardama in the shelter of the tree branches. Two Dasai tribesmen approached, bearing a small covered litter between them. On it lay Archana and Calum.

Sarah knelt beside the spirit-wounded batlings in the falling rain. 'Hello, dear friends,' she said softly, and she gently stroked their fur. The batlings hummed contentedly.

'We're sorry we weren't able to warn you in time,' Archana said in a faint whisper.

'Hush,' said Sarah. 'You were the best scouts I could have asked for.'

Rein joined her and said, 'You two must save your strength and concentrate on getting well.'

Tor stepped forward and shouted above the rain, 'I went back in the night to tell the people you were leaving. We all came to see you off.' He turned to Rein and clasped his arm. ''Tis a fair match made this day! See she's back before too long!'

A feeling of dread filled Sarah, and she sought Marwa in the crowd. He was there by the old tree, which was still twisted, but lush now with a crown of green leaves.

She ran to him, and threw herself into his arms. 'Will I be able to get back to Hutanya when I want to?' she called to him over the downpour. 'Will I remember?'

'Yes and no, child,' Marwa replied. 'You'll be able to come through the door when it is time. You're leaving of your own free will, so the door will always open for you again. And when you do come back you will remember all that has happened since you began the quest. But when you are in the land beyond, I don't know what you will remember. I only know that you will be back.' The wizard held her tightly and said in the Old Tongue, '*San bu kanca na bie.*' It was the blessing he had given Will and her before they had begun the quest. Now she knew what it meant. *I will hold you in the light.*

'*San ku kana na lie,*' she replied. *And so I hold you.*

And then Rein was beside her, holding her in a crushing embrace. This time his kiss told her far more of the depth of his love. He released her and said, 'I will be waiting for you.'

Sarah lifted the kalu pendant and brought it to her lips. Its song was as sweet as any promise, like sleigh bells and meadow larks, ringing and singing together. She smiled into Rein's dark eyes. 'Remember what we spoke of last night. I too will be sad if you don't celebrate the new life until I return. It won't be so long. I promise.'

Then Marwa called, 'The door!'

They turned to see the shimmer of green light as the door took shape beneath the old tree. Sarah reached out and linked her fingers with Rein's, and he brought her hand swiftly to his lips before releasing her. The rain was cool, but the place where his lips had touched her hand stayed warm. She smiled her promise into Rein's eyes until she saw what she was looking for in them. When he finally smiled back, she knew he believed she would come again.

Then she turned to Marwa.

'Farewell, sweet child,' the old wizard said, as he held her close. 'It is time to go.'

Sarah turned to look at the people, the batlings and grazels and the cardamas, all gathered in the falling rain. She raised her palms to the sky, and then turned and laid them on the face of the door. The carvings of cats and other creatures were familiar now; Sarah recognised the taywa and the ilix, and the bird, Myra, as she touched the gold serpent in the centre of the door. And then the humming began, soon drowning out the pouring rain as the door swung open and the rushing river appeared beyond its threshold. Sarah thought of Will, of his bright sunny smile.

'Farewell, little friend,' she whispered, and then she did not hesitate. She plunged head first into the water.

THIRTY-TWO

Sarah awoke to the soft whooshing sound of a door swinging open. It was dark, and there was a dull throbbing in her head. She could hear the distant rumble of thunder beyond the drawn curtains. She was thirsty, and as she struggled up to a sitting position, a bedside lamp was switched on, lighting her parents' faces as they sat together next to her bed.

'Hi, honey,' said her mother softly.

'You gave us quite a scare, Sarah Clare,' said her father, hugging her gently.

Sarah must have looked blank, because her mother asked, 'Do you remember what happened, honey? We found you on the floor in the greenhouse.'

'I hit my head on a hanging pot,' said Sarah.

Behind her parents, Sarah could see the doctor whose entrance had woken her. He came forward and examined her quickly and efficiently before pronouncing, 'She appears to be fine. There doesn't seem to be any concussion, although I must say I'm surprised. A blow hard enough to knock her unconscious ...'

Sarah closed her eyes as the doctor murmured instructions to her parents. *I'm back*, she thought, and the knowledge was bittersweet. Her hand crept to her neck, where she felt the fine gold chain inside her blouse. She wondered what her parents would say if she told them what had really happened. *They'd probably think I was dreaming, or suffering delusions from the bump on my head*, she thought.

'Where's Aunt Jenny?' she asked, suddenly. Her parents looked at one another, and then grinned at her. 'There's been all kinds of excitement today,' said her father with a twinkle in his eyes.

'The doctor says we can take you home. Would you like to see Aunt Jenny before we go?'

'She's here?' asked Sarah, swinging her legs over the side of the bed.

'Slowly, now, honey,' warned her father. He swung her up in his arms, and Sarah felt once again like the child she had been before her journey. 'And no questions!' he commanded. 'I don't think I can talk and carry you at the same time! OUFF! Have you been growing again?' he teased, as they pushed out the door.

Her father put her down outside a room on the fourth floor. 'Go on in, Sarah,' said her mother. 'We'll need to sign some papers, and then we'll be back for you.'

Sarah entered the room. The hissing of car tyres on the wet street outside was the only sound. Her aunt lay in the single bed, her long hair tousled on the pillow. A slight smile curled her lips, and Sarah tiptoed over to take a closer look at her. Aunt Jenny was sound asleep. Sarah sat down in the rocking chair by the bed.

She was startled by the door swinging open, as a large, ruddy-faced nurse swept into the room carrying a tiny bundle in her arms. She eyed Sarah suspiciously, and then bent over a crib Sarah had failed to notice and laid the bundle down. Sarah heard the nurse draw in her breath sharply, and she flashed the girl an angry look.

'What's this?' she hissed indignantly, holding up the green tendril of a plant.

Aunt Jenny stirred in her sleep, which silenced the nurse, but Sarah could tell by the woman's pursed lips that she was not pleased with Sarah's presence. The nurse fussed around the crib, gave Sarah a final disapproving glare, and swept out the door.

There was no sound from the crib. Sarah rose from the rocking chair and slowly approached the high bed. She was aware of a powdery, warm scent. She peered over the edge of the white lace trimming.

Within lay a baby, a tiny pale child with faint roses of pink on his cheeks. He was so beautiful that Sarah caught her breath in wonder. Downy white fuzz crowned his head, and his rosebud lips were slightly parted. His nose was a tiny snub, and his small fist was tucked up beside it. As Sarah bent closer, entranced, she felt a faint coolness rising to greet her. She reached in and gently caressed his little hand. The sleeping baby's fingers unfurled to reveal a delicate pearly shell. Sarah gasped, then gently lifted the kalu to read the rune engraved on it.

It said *rainbow*.

Aunt Jenny stirred on the bed behind her. 'What do you think of your new cousin?' her aunt asked sleepily.

The baby's eyes fluttered open at the sound of his mother's voice. Jade pools reflected Sarah's eyes back at her, which were welling with joyful tears.

'He's perfect,' whispered Sarah, her gaze fastened on the beloved face of her small friend. Aunt Jenny put her arms around Sarah as they both looked at the baby.

'I'm sorry I'll have to return to the research station so soon,' said Aunt Jenny. 'I want you two to know each other well. Your parents have promised to bring you for a visit next year.'

'That's all right,' Sarah said. 'He'll be where he belongs. He'll love it there.'

Aunt Jenny's warm breath brushed her hair. 'I think so, too. There will be so much for him to explore and to learn.'

Sarah remembered the dry, barren desert of Karst before the waters were freed. She thought about Sarin's threat to her own world. 'I have a lot to learn, too. I've realised how important the work you do is. I want to help.'

Aunt Jenny laughed and held her close. 'I believe you do! You'd be surprised at how much difference one person can make if she's determined to accomplish something.'

Sarah was silent, remembering her quest. A thin ray of sunlight broke through the dark clouds that hovered at the window and laid a prism of shimmering colour on the wall. Sarah saw a small lizard scuttle across it and disappear into the shadows.

'What shall we call him, honey?' Aunt Jenny rested her cheek lightly against Sarah's head. They looked down at the baby, who waved his tiny fists at them.

Sarah smiled. 'Will,' she said.

'Will.' Aunt Jenny studied the child, as though measuring the name against him. 'Not William or Bill?' She lifted the baby, and deposited him gently in Sarah's arms.

Sarah stroked one tiny foot. The baby cooed softly, and the sound rippled around them like a pebble dropping into a still pool. She kissed his cool cheek, and raised her head to meet Aunt Jenny's thoughtful gaze.

'No,' Sarah replied decisively, her heart alight with fierce love. 'Just Will.'